They were close, very close

Alone, for the moment, in the rich green world of the nursery, canopied by the dazzling blue sky. Slowly, his eyes darkening, Alex drew Jo toward him. And as that deeply implanted warning— business and pleasure don't mix—buzzed in her mind, Jo made the conscious effort to ignore it.

Perhaps it would prove foolish, perhaps insane, but she didn't want to resist Alex. Very deliberately, he took her in his arms, then bent to claim her mouth with his.

His kiss was velvet. Deep and warm and incredibly stirring. As Jo's senses swam, as those built-in inhibitions began to melt away, she let pure instinct replace her usual logic. And when he began to draw away, she couldn't bear to let him go.

Wordlessly, by the eloquence of her eyes and the urgency of her hands pressing against his shoulders, she invited him back again....

Dear Reader,

Each and every month, to meet your sophisticated standards, to satisfy your taste for substantial, memorable, emotion-packed novels of life and love, of dreams and possibilities, Silhouette brings you six extremely **Special Editions**.

Soon these exclusive editions will sport a new, updated cover look—our way of marking Silhouette **Special Editions'** continually renewed commitment to bring you the very best and the brightest in romance writing.

Keep an eye out for the new Silhouette **Special Edition** covers—inside you'll find a soul-satisfying selection of love stories penned by your favorite Silhouette authors and by some dazzling new writers destined to become tomorrow's romance stars.

And don't forget the two Silhouette *Classics* at your bookseller's each month—the most beloved Silhouette **Special Editions** and Silhouette *Intimate Moments* of yesteryear, now reissued by popular demand.

Today's bestsellers, tomorrow's *Classics*—that's Silhouette **Special Editions**. And soon, we'll be looking more special than ever!

From all the authors and editors of Silhouette **Special Editions**,

Warmest Wishes,

Leslie Kazanjian
Senior Editor

MAGGI CHARLES
It Must Be Magic

Silhouette Special Edition

Published by Silhouette Books New York

America's Publisher of Contemporary Romance

To Craig and Vicky...
with warm and wonderful memories
of a Saturday in San Juan...
and the Pink Palace.

SILHOUETTE BOOKS
300 East 42nd St., New York, N.Y. 10017

ISBN: 0-373-09479-5

First Silhouette Books printing September 1988

Printed in the U.S.A.

MAGGI CHARLES

is a confirmed traveler who readily admits that "people and places fascinate me." A prolific author, who is also known to her romance fans as Meg Hudson, Ms. Charles states that if she hadn't become a writer she would have been a musician, having studied piano and harp. A native New Yorker, she is the mother of two sons and currently resides in Cape Cod, Massachusetts, with her husband.

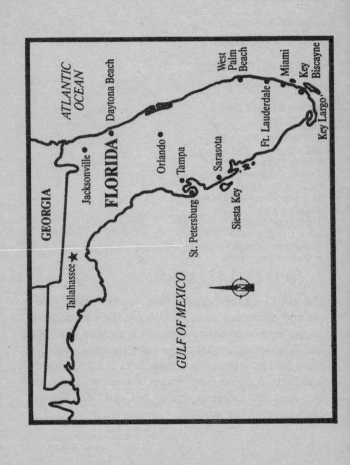

Chapter One

"Jo, it's that man again."

Josephine Bennett glanced up from the stack of invoices she was scanning. As she worked, she'd been reflecting that Greenscapes, Inc. seemed to be on the verge of something really big. So much business! New shopping malls, new restaurants, new condominiums, new enterprises of all sizes, sorts and descriptions...and they all wanted professionally maintained greenery to adorn their premises.

It was a marvel, a miracle. Even her father, who'd had complete faith in the future of what he'd termed "natural decorating" would have found his company's spiraling success hard to believe. He would have been so proud.

Clark Bennett had been gone two years, but Jo still missed him terribly—both at the helm of the family business and as the father she'd dearly loved. She sighed regretfully as she turned to face her secretary, who was waiting patiently in the doorway.

"Sorry, Marge. What did you say? My mind was elsewhere."

"That man is on the phone again. Alex Grant, that is. This is the fifth time he's called, Jo. Each time I explained that you were either out of the building or tied up with something, and each time he's sounded angrier. Right now, he's sizzling!"

Jo stacked the invoices. Setting them to one side she asked, "What's it about, do you know?"

"I have no idea," Marge responded. "He insists on discussing whatever it is with you personally."

Jo hesitated, tempted to tell her secretary to stall the man till tomorrow. It had been a full day and, the way things were going, she wouldn't be leaving the nursery until well after dark. She'd spent the morning with several clients who'd wanted to view Greenscapes' extensive grounds. Then there had been a business lunch in nearby Bradenton with people who were opening a large Mexican restaurant, a franchise operation. They needed an exotic natural decor to complement the restaurant's Spanish courtyard interior. If Jo landed their account, she'd be getting the company's future business as more franchises opened in the area. So she'd put her very best foot forward, and was reasonably sure she'd soon be receiving a call from the restaurateurs to confirm the assignment.

Lunch had lasted well into the afternoon. Back in her office, she'd immediately tackled the paperwork that was piled up on her desk, and was just beginning to make a dent in it. It wasn't a good time for an interruption, especially from an angry man she didn't even know.

"What did you say his name was, Marge?"

"Alex Grant."

It didn't ring a bell.

Jo grimaced, knowing there was seldom any benefit in putting off petty annoyances.

"Tell Mr. Grant I'll be right with him," she said abruptly, then added with a wry smile, "Give me a few seconds to polish my phone voice, okay?"

Marge nodded agreement and went back to her desk. A moment later, when Jo spoke into the phone, her tone was exactly right. Apologetic, but not too apologetic. Brisk, but not too brisk. Pleasant, conveying interest in the caller, but also making it clear that she was a very busy woman who had no time for grievances that didn't concern her. If this man were a client, it would be different. Any client's displeasure concerned her deeply. As it was . . .

"Mr. Grant? Sorry to keep you waiting," she murmured.

Thunder cannot be transmitted via telephone, nor is silence necessarily ominous. Hidden tension doesn't always spin cobwebs of disquiet. So why, Jo asked herself, was she hearing thunder, shivering through the following silence, then feeling herself caught by invisible cobwebs as their threads were drawn tighter and tighter?

"Mr. Grant?" she repeated.

"This *is* Miss Bennett?"

The deep, husky voice dripped sarcasm. Jo fought back an instinctive sharp retort and said, "Yes, this is Miss Bennett."

"I was beginning to wonder if there really was one," Alex Grant told her. "I was about to conclude that you were a company logo."

"What?"

"Like Betty Crocker, Aunt Jemima.... Shall I go on?"

"I don't think that's necessary," Jo answered smoothly. "As I said, I'm sorry we didn't connect sooner. Perhaps you could tell me why you wanted to contact me?"

"I'd be delighted to." The husky voice was suspiciously polite. "In fact, I postponed my flight out of Sarasota-Bradenton Airport until tomorrow just to show you personally why I've taken the time and trouble to reach you, Miss Bennett. Get in your car and trundle along to my office, and I think what you see will be clear enough to satisfy you."

Patiently she said, "It's rather late in the day, Mr. Grant, and I have no idea where your office is. Even if I did, I don't have time to meet with you on the spur of the moment. I have an equally full agenda tomorrow, I might add."

"Agendas can be revised, Miss Bennett," the husky voice informed her. "Have you been over to the Mimosa Mall recently?"

"The Mimosa Mall won't be open for another week," Jo pointed out, her annoyance beginning to seep through her words.

"Quite true. But Greenscapes, Inc. did the plants for the mall, did they not?" Alex Grant persisted gruffly. "That's to say, your firm designed and installed the interior plantscape, didn't it? And you are under contract to maintain those plants, correct?"

"Yes," Jo agreed...and later wondered why warning bells didn't start to ring wildly at that point.

"Then," Alex Grant said, "let me again suggest that you head for my office as quickly as possible. I trust my company will be more readily familiar to you than I am. Malls International, Ltd. You have heard of us, haven't you?"

He could not have been more sarcastic. Still, Jo grew weak at the knees as she heard what he was saying. Sarcastic or not, Alex Grant was Greenscapes' most important current client, and a new one to boot! She berated herself for not recognizing the name Grant. But "Alex" Grant hadn't meant a thing to her. She'd never met the president of Malls International, whom she knew of simply as Danforth A. Grant.

At the time the account had been secured, Jo had been in Miami opening a branch of Greenscapes on Florida's east coast. Her cousin Tim had negotiated the account, but with a representative of Malls International, not the president. Jo wished fervently that Tim, now manager of Greenscapes' new Miami office, was back here in Las Flores so he could take this particular flack himself!

As she agreed to meet Alex Grant at the Mimosa Mall as soon as she could get there, Jo wondered, her apprehension mounting, what possibly could have gone wrong. She'd personally surveyed the premises three weeks before, the day the foliage design plan was completed and the plants, trees and shrubs were in place. The mall was enormous, and it had taken a high degree of expertise on the part of Jo and her staff to achieve the lush, green tropical illusion the client wanted.

At the time, she remembered, Danforth Grant had been in Italy, presiding at the opening of a new mall constructed by his company outside Rome. Now she wished bitterly he'd stayed there!

The Mimosa Mall bridged the Sarasota-Bradenton line a few miles east of both cities. It was rightfully being publicized as the largest mall on the Florida Gulf Coast, covering nearly one hundred and thirty acres. Five huge department stores anchored one hundred and sixty specialty shops and eateries, all enclosed in an impressive and inviting complex. There was an exotic, Byzantine emphasis to the architecture, highlighted by a large glass dome that covered a central pedestrian rotunda. This spacious, high-walled area combined an interior park with half a dozen "outdoor" cafés, behind which wide corridors radiated like spokes from a wheel, each lined with one-of-a-kind boutiques. Appropriately, the corridor sectors were known as The Bazaars. Each had been given a name that would have pleased Scheherazade, as they were taken straight from the pages of her famed *Arabian Nights*.

The mall's exterior was done in muted tans, pinks, greens and aquas, and the overall effect was enchanting. When she'd last viewed the mall, Jo had really felt excited about this project. In her opinion, Greenscapes had more than done its share in the successful realization of the mall. The verdant park beneath the huge glass dome had, she'd thought proudly, surely emerged as the most beautiful oasis any weary desert traveler could ever expect to find.

With her last visit still in mind, she strode toward the magnificent rotunda, the mall's focal point, confident that Greenscapes could not possibly have done a better job. Then shock rooted her to the colorful mosaic tiles underfoot, and she gasped, unable to believe what she was seeing.

Everything about the rotunda was perfect—except the plantscape. From where she stood, Jo saw drooping trees, yellowing plants and withering shrubs. It was as if winterkill had struck at the very heart of this perfectly controlled, man-made climate. Any resemblance to the kind of oasis camel riders dream about was gone!

Faced with the ruin of her company's work, she shriveled inwardly, wishing she were enough of a coward to turn tail and run. But running was hardly her style, personally or professionally. Still, the thought of facing Alex Grant was too ghastly to contemplate.

Jo squared her shoulders as she tried to gather her thoughts. It was at that moment that she became aware of the man watching her from a shadowy alcove beyond one of the cafés. She was not often given to premonitions, but the sudden sinking feeling that she wouldn't have to go very far to find the mall's owner was overwhelming.

He came slowly toward her. Jo stood her ground. She was slightly nearsighted—she wore glasses for driving and the movies—so he was fairly close to her before his features became really distinct.

Focusing on his face, Jo nearly gasped a second time. Years had passed—about a dozen, she calculated rapidly—and he looked older, to be sure. He'd had his hair cut, and was wearing a conservative business suit instead of the trademark jeans, tie-dyed T-shirt and beads strung around his neck. Probably a lot of the people who'd been his followers back then wouldn't even recognize him now, she conceded. But she would have known him anywhere, because she'd been passionately in love with him.

Danny Forth. He'd been going by that name about the time she started high school. A rock star who, unfortunately, had never toured near enough to Sarasota for Jo to see him in concert. So she'd squandered her allowance on his movies, and still vividly remembered those Saturday afternoons spent in whatever area theater Danny Forth's pictures were being shown, gazing at him soulfully through her oversize horn-rims.

She'd spent the balance of her allowance on his albums. She still had them. In fact, she'd rediscovered them a year ago when she'd converted the family home—a rambling old farmhouse adjacent to the nursery—into additional offices, because it was just too lonely to continue living there by herself. Now the albums were stashed away on a closet shelf in her condo overlooking Sarasota Bay.

Years had passed since she'd last played a Danny Forth record—years since the star himself had faded from the spotlight, as even the brightest stars in entertainment's fickle sky so often do. It had been years since she'd even heard of him. Facing him now, she inadvertently took a step backward. She hadn't realized how tall he was. He'd also filled out considerably, though she doubted there was a spare ounce of fat on his body, from what she could see. He looked very fit, and considerably more athletic than she would have expected.

"Miss Bennett?" he asked. "I'm Alex Grant." His husky voice was distinctive, different.

He hadn't sounded like that back in his guitar swinging, rock singing days, and curiosity stirred. Somewhere at the back of her mind a small fact was stored, but though she tried, she couldn't budge it.

It'll come to me later, she promised herself. Then she slammed the door on the past and faced up to the present.

Again she surveyed the once-stunning rotunda of this man's mall. Looking him right in the eye, she said, "Frankly, I don't know what to say to you. I can't imagine what's happened. These plants have only been here for three weeks. I checked before I left the office. They were serviced last Monday, and are scheduled to be serviced again tomorrow."

"I think," Alex Grant informed her, "that 'replaced' might be a better word."

Jo wasn't about to quibble with his assessment. Most of the plants and trees in the rotunda would obviously have to be replaced. She only hoped they could be coaxed back to health at the nursery. Otherwise, the dollar loss involved was going to be awesome. But the loss of prestige for Greenscapes, Inc. would be even greater—and far harder to recoup.

"This is only the beginning," he went on. He glanced over her head toward one of the wide corridors, and suggested, "Shall we take a walk?"

Jo nodded reluctantly. "I suppose we'd better."

They started out, side by side, in silence. Jo, trying to keep pace, felt like a small, chastised child. Though she was almost five foot five, Alex Grant seemed to tower over her. She felt overpowered by him, or was it overwhelmed? More than anything, she was very disconcerted to realize that it was possible to dislike on sight someone you'd once blindly adored.

He exuded no particular charisma as they walked along together—and he'd possessed the ultimate in charisma back in those earlier years. Now he was all business. This was clearly to Jo's advantage. Her professional senses swung into action, pushing aside her momentary sense of inadequacy.

Something, something she couldn't put into words began to bother her. She sniffed as if she were actually smelling trouble, then realized that the problem didn't involve scent. It was a question of sight.

She stopped near a rectangular patio where a fountain splashed plumes of crystal-blue water into a gorgeous mosaic tile basin. It was a jewel of a spot, so beautifully executed that Jo's heart had skipped a few beats when she'd viewed it three weeks ago. Now the fountain seemed surprisingly desolate. Again, like an oasis gone wrong.

Why? Jo demanded silently, her agony mounting. *Why?*

Suddenly the answer came to her. It was so obvious that she couldn't imagine how she'd missed latching onto the difference immediately. But she did so now, and whirled to face Alex Grant, her resentment emerging in a laserlike flash of anger.

He was only a step or two away from her, so close that she literally bumped into him. Instantly she recoiled, her dark brown eyes narrowing as she exclaimed, "It's the lighting, that's what's wrong! What have you done to it?"

Before Alex Grant could answer, Jo tilted back her head and stared up at the ceiling, a considerable distance, as they were cathedral-high. After squinting for a moment, she reached into her handbag, whipped out her glasses, then stared anew.

"As I thought," she declared triumphantly. "You've covered all the skylights."

"Not covered," Alex Grant corrected. "Painted over."

"Painted over?" Jo echoed, clearly conveying her horror.

"That's what I said, Miss Bennett," he nodded, then added innocently, "What's so wrong with that?"

Jo took off her glasses, too choked with anger to respond to his question. She moved to the nearest grouping of shrubs and carefully fingered the leaves. Several dropped off without further encouragement. Then she turned—and Alex Grant found himself the subject of brown eyes so scathing that they made him want to wriggle.

That was something he couldn't remember ever doing. He stared down at Josephine Bennett, amazed that she could evoke such a response from him. Since walking into the mall this morning and surveying veritable acres of dying plants, shrubs and magnificent specimen trees, he'd worked up a definite hostility toward her. Now he felt that hostility rapidly fading away.

She was quite lovely to look at, Alex discovered. He grabbed the opportunity to study her when she turned back to her plants, too absorbed with inspecting yel-

lowing leaves to notice him. She was a bit on the short
side, yet not petite. Nor was she pretty in the conven-
tional sense. Rather, Josephine Bennett was touched
with a more lasting brand of beauty, one that would
only improve with time and maturity. And there was
a latent sexiness about her. He suspected maybe she
was unaware of just how provocative she was, especially when she was presenting an all-business facade.

He liked her perfect little nose, the gentle curve of
her cheeks, the fullness of her pale pink mouth. Her
shoulder-length hair was almost exactly the color of
amber. An interesting contrast to those expressive dark
eyes. But it was the more subtle things, not readily
defined, that piqued his curiosity.

He estimated she was in her late twenties. Several
years younger than he was. That was young to be
running one of the largest foliage design companies in
Florida.

She still hadn't told him what was so wrong with
painting the numerous glass skylights the cool shade
of turquoise that in his opinion made the mall's interior so much more inviting. He asked again, "Was
there something wrong with painting the skylights?"

For a moment, Jo looked at Alex Grant in a way
that made him feel she doubted his intelligence. Then
she said, "I'm surprised you didn't stop to realize
what you were doing. Shutting out light. Vital light."
She glanced around, shaking her head in disbelief.
"You can see the results for yourself, Mr. Grant. Most
indoor plants and shrubs and trees require bright light.
Lots of bright light. It can be natural or artificial, that
doesn't matter. What does matter is that you provide
at least as much light as these plants would receive

outdoors. There are two musts in horticulture—light and water. These plants all look as though they've been overwatered, which I can assure you is not the fault of my company. What kind of paint did you use, anyway?'' she demanded.

"Opaque," Alex muttered. "I can't tell you precisely the kind. I told my manager...Craig Franey, do you know him?"

"Yes, we've met."

"Well, I told Craig the effect I wanted, and he ordered the work done. That was when I was here last, about a month ago, right before you installed the plants. I guess they didn't get around to the actual painting until your people had finished their work and left."

"Definitely not, or we wouldn't have planted."

"Miss Bennett?"

"Yes?"

It was a long time since Alex had done much apologizing to anyone, a long time since he'd needed to. He was extremely careful in his business affairs and allowed no leeway for mistakes on either his part of anyone else's. As for his personal affairs...

He blocked that avenue of thought.

"Miss Bennett," he began again.

"Mr. Grant," she countered, with exaggerated politeness.

"I know I came on strong," Alex admitted, aware that this young woman had absolutely no idea how much of an admission that was for him. "And...I'm sorry. I shouldn't have leapt to conclusions."

"It's understandable," Jo allowed. "I obviously didn't recognize your nickname, but once you'd identified yourself, I began to recall all those business articles I've read about Danforth Grant's astuteness.''

A faint smile tugged at the corners of Alex's mouth. "You can't believe everything you read, Miss Bennett," he protested mildly.

Jo caught that hint of a smile, and was instantly claimed by the ghost of memories past. On screen, his lopsided grin had been the most provocative expression she'd ever seen on anyone's face. And those discerning slate-gray eyes...

Questions suddenly tumbled into her head. True, stars faded. But it seemed in retrospect that Danny Forth had faded more rapidly than most. She'd lost track of him while she was in college, giving serious attention to the study of plants and their pathology. Then she'd emerged into the world again, a more contemporary world with new stars, new attractions. To be honest, she'd not thought too much about Danny Forth. He'd become part of her teen past, like blowing huge bubbles of gum, drinking god-awful sweet wine and wearing the latest wild fads...and taking so much for granted.

Like the things that really mattered, Jo thought ruefully. Like home and family and love.

She'd learned early the hard side of taking things for granted. Way before she'd reached her teens. She'd only been eight when her brother Bob had been killed in Vietnam. Had it not been for that, there was no telling what she might have done. Become a ballet dancer, maybe? An actress? An archaeologist? She'd gone through a phase in which she'd done a lot of fantasizing about unearthing ancient tombs filled with treasure.

But as things stood, even during the crazy teen years, Jo had known quite clearly what she would do with her life. She would carry on with Greenscapes. She had detoured only once when, right after graduation, she'd eloped with Jim Lansing, the football star of her high school class. They'd driven all the way to Alabama to get married. Ironically, it had been Jim's family, not hers, that had forced the subsequent annulment.

The Lansings' main concern had been that Jo might be pregnant. To this day she had no idea what course they would have followed had that proved to be the case.

"Miss Bennett?" Alex Grant nudged politely.

Jo gathered in the mental wool she'd been unraveling. "I'm sorry," she apologized. "I was thinking about . . . all this."

As her gaze encompassed the scene in the mall, it also took in the tall man standing next to her. Certainly he must have a devoted London tailor. His light gray suit could not have fitted him more perfectly. He also had an excellent hair stylist who knew exactly how to shape his thick, near-black hair neatly to his head. In Danny Forth's rock 'n' roll days, his hair had tumbled wildly to his shoulders, she recalled.

He was still waiting politely for her to make a comment. She glanced up into cool eyes that appeared gray one moment and blue the next, watched a dark eyebrow arch ever so slightly, and suddenly sensed that this man could be an extremely powerful adversary.

He's been tried and tested, she found herself thinking. *And now he's forged out of pure steel.*

Carefully she said, "I think the blame for this fiasco must be placed on your shoulders, Mr. Grant."

She caught a glimpse of something in his blue-gray eyes, was tempted to identify it as admiration, then warned herself not to take his slight lapse as a sign that she'd gained the upper hand. She waited for his reaction, and couldn't repress her surprise when he merely asked, "Perhaps you could elaborate on that?"

Maybe it was his closeness to her. She could smell his fresh scent, a blend of soap and after-shave. Maybe it was the intensity of the way he was looking at her, as if he deeply cared about hearing her answer. Maybe it was teenage memories resurfacing. Maybe she was beginning to realize how much she'd underrated his current charisma. Whatever it was, Jo was dismayed to feel a sudden throb of pure sensuality assault her.

She managed to control her voice and to sound very businesslike as she said, "As I've told you, all plants need light. Lots of light. By painting those skylights, you shut off major sources of that much-needed light. Didn't you stop to realize your architect had incorporated all that glass into his design for a specific reason? So he could give you the kind of oasis effects you must have asked for?"

Alex nodded. "That's true enough."

"Well?"

He frowned, then said, "There was a reason why I ordered the paint job done. It was necessary to solve a problem."

"What problem?"

"When I came in here a month ago it was early afternoon. I walked into the rotunda and the sun nearly blinded me. The rays were shooting down through the skylights, blazing right into my eyes. I found it a nuisance, and I imagined many mall patrons would, too. So it occurred to me that the subtle use of paint could diffuse the sun's rays and create a more subdued effect. One more pleasing, and infinitely more comfortable.''

Alex Grant paused and slowly shook his head. Then, to Jo's astonishment, he favored her with that incredibly appealing lopsided grin. "So," he finished, with disarming simplicity, "I guess I goofed."

Chapter Two

Jo was so mesmerized by Alex Grant that she couldn't answer him. His smile was sending her straight back to her teens. And his admission was the last thing she'd expected to hear from the owner of Malls International, Ltd.

Somewhat grudgingly, she conceded that a man who so readily admitted a major mistake couldn't be as hard and unrelenting as this acknowledgedly successful businessman had first appeared. Maybe she'd been a little hasty in her initial evaluation. She didn't doubt he possessed plenty of steel. Instinctively she knew it would be a mistake to underrate him in that respect. But the vibes she was feeling toward him now suggested that the steel was tempered by some far more appealing human qualities.

He was looking at her in a disturbingly sexy way. Maybe it was a trick of the lighting, but those slate eyes of his were surprisingly warm.

Hesitantly she said, "Maybe we both goofed. Before I left my office, I checked the records. I can understand why our man in charge of maintenance for this project didn't find anything wrong the first week. But the second time around I would think he might have noticed that the foliage wasn't doing as well as it should have been."

Thinking this through, Jo frowned. Len Faraday headed the crew responsible for the Mimosa Mall, and there was no one in the nursery business she trusted more. Len had been in plant care and maintenance for years, and had joined Greenscapes shortly after her father founded the firm. She couldn't imagine Len not noticing every last detail about a project, especially one this important.

She studied a sadly drooping plant and grimaced. "Regardless of who's to blame," she went on, "this is a mess. We'll get on it immediately, Mr. Grant. But there is one proviso."

"Yes?"

"You're going to have to remove that paint from the skylights. Otherwise the same thing will happen all over again."

Alex Grant folded his arms and considered that. After a long moment, he said, "I don't want to be stubborn, Miss Bennett, but I really don't want to do that. To my mind, the sunlight was much too glaring."

"You saw all this before we did the plantscape," Jo reminded him, as they started back toward the rotunda. "The foliage softened the harsh light, even when it was at its brightest. I can assure you of that. I inspected the work myself the day it was completed and came back the next day to recheck. It was a sunny day, and the effect was like gold filtering into a rain forest. It was really enchanting." She flashed him an impish grin, and added, "I didn't even need to put on my sunglasses."

He didn't return the grin, didn't immediately answer her. Rather, he leaned backward and stared up at the lofty, glass-paned dome. Abruptly he decided, "I think we need to talk this over. I don't have an office per se in the mall, Miss Bennett, despite my request over the phone that you hurry over here. Our company headquarters are in New York, so I spend most of my office time there. A great deal of my work, however, involves traveling from one location to the next. Generally speaking, I use the premises of the local manager in our various malls. In this case, Craig Franey's office. We could talk in there, I suppose. But Craig already feels pretty bad about this."

"It wasn't his fault," Jo said automatically.

"I know, but he doesn't quite see it that way." Alex Grant's lopsided smile flashed briefly. "I guess I came down rather hard on him," he admitted. "When I walked in here first thing this morning... well, I was staggered. If someone had deliberately set out to sabotage us, they couldn't have done a better job. So my initial outburst was directed at Craig. I felt he should have seen what was happening and done something to correct it immediately. Now that I think of it, he did say he thought some of the plants seemed to be dying."

"Did he call the nursery?"

"Yes, he did. He said he talked to a Len Faraday. Evidently he handles the plant maintenance."

"That's right."

"I can't quote exactly what your man told Craig, but I gather the gist of it was that he felt this must be a temporary setback that could easily be remedied. Evidently Mr. Faraday felt everything was fine when his crew made their routine check last Monday, as you said. He promised to come with the crew himself tomorrow, and Craig was content to let it go at that. Obviously, I wasn't."

Jo felt a twinge of sympathy for Craig Franey. They'd had a few meetings to discuss the design for the plantscape and coordinate its installation with the other phases of the mall's development. She'd found him a pleasant and agreeable middle-aged man. Capable, thoroughly knowledgeable about his work. But no match, she thought wryly, for Mall International's owner!

"Anyway," Alex Grant continued, "I'd suggest we go somewhere else to have our talk."

"We can use my office, if you like," Jo offered. "Las Flores is only twenty minutes from here."

Alex Grant glanced at his slim gold wristwatch. "How about adjourning to a quiet cocktail lounge?" he suggested. "It is that time of day."

Jo was tempted to tell him that there were few quiet spots to be found along Florida's Gulf Coast in the middle of March. It was the height of the tourist season, and all the clubs and restaurants that came to mind would be packed at this hour. She racked her brain for a place that would not be noisy and crowded.

Before she could come up with anything, Alex said casually, "I have a suite at the Floridiana. Why don't we go there?"

Jo hesitated. The Floridiana was a new hotel in downtown Sarasota, just across the street from the harbor. She'd been there for dinner one night with friends and had found it a shade overdone for her taste. Too much vivid pink, too many palms, too many ceramic flamingos, too staged a tropical setting. All they needed was their own polished moon to hang up in a plastic sky.

She was rather surprised that Alex Grant had chosen the Floridiana to stay at. It cast light on another aspect of his character. Perhaps he actually liked the "pseudo" settings that so often went with life in the fast lane, right down to the last bit of fake Deco decor.

"As it happens," he explained, as though he could read her mind, "I bought into the place. When I saw the place yesterday, I almost wished I hadn't. But I have to admit it's practically guaranteed to be a profitable investment."

She had to smile at that. "I think we might do better in a smaller place I've just remembered. It's about five miles from here in an area not quite so familiar to the tourists. I'm sure we can find a quiet booth there."

"As you wish," Alex agreed. "Suppose you lead the way and I'll follow."

He was driving a modest rental car, Jo noticed. Again she was surprised. She would have expected him to want something much flashier or at least more expensive. Maybe a Porsche or Mercedes, she decided, as she carefully negotiated her way through the early-evening traffic. But with each mile she found it increasingly difficult to concentrate on her driving. She was becoming more and more conscious of the man at the wheel of the car just behind her.

If it hadn't been for that slightly lopsided smile and that disarming admission that he'd "goofed," she would have put Alex Grant down as a very attractive yet rather classic, contemporary example of a rich and successful American businessman. He certainly looked the type. She could picture him whisking around the country in his private jet, possibly taking the controls himself when the mood struck. She could imagine him leading a glittering social life with a gorgeous, perfect-in-every-way wife acting as his hostess. She could envision him appearing consummately at ease in the international settings to which his work took him. She could see him excelling in everything he did, from playing a smashing game of tennis to creating a perfect martini. Performing with grace, charm and finesse. But performing, as Danny Forth once had. Living life onstage.

Underneath the veneer, Jo would have said that someone like Danforth A. Grant had a calculator for a mind and a computer for a heart. But the lopsided grin, the almost boyish admission, had dented that notion.

They pulled up side by side in the parking lot of the small club she'd chosen. She hoped the place would not yet be crowded, and it wasn't. They found a corner booth, and Alex ordered bourbon, while Jo favored blush wine. Music created a background filter, the lights were low. Though it was too late to make a change, Jo wished she'd selected another locale. This setting was a little too intimate, too conducive to re-laxing. It would be easy to forget the real purpose of their rendezvous.

"About the plantscape," she began, determined to zero in on business before she became sidetracked.

Alex chuckled. "Right," he agreed. He sipped his drink, then said, "When Craig Franey showed me our contract with your company and I saw it was signed J.A. Bennett, President, I assumed you were a man. The assumption seemed to be verified when I heard you referred to as Jo Bennett. It wasn't until your secretary kept telling me that Miss Bennett was not available to come to the phone that I realized my er-ror."

"I'd call that an honest mistake, not an error."

"Is Jo short for Josephine?"

"Yes," she nodded. "And before you ask, I'll tell you. The *A* is for Angela." She tasted her wine, then said, "While we're on the subject of names..."

"Yes?"

"Well, you didn't exactly identify yourself as Dan-forth A. Grant. If you had, my secretary would have immediately recognized who you were."

"And you would have come to the phone sooner?"

"I'm afraid not," Jo told him honestly. "I really wasn't available when you called. But at least I would have known it was really important. I might have even quaked accordingly," she teased.

"It's not my purpose to make people quake, Jo."

Alex spoke her first name casually, but Jo's heart thumped nonetheless. It was difficult to believe she actually was sitting across from her teenage heart-throb in a scene she would never have dared to dream up.

"Sometimes," Alex added huskily, "I make waves despite myself, but that's seldom my intention."

"I'll buy that," Jo managed, then quickly sipped her wine again, keenly aware of how dry her throat had suddenly become.

"Let me ask you something, though," he persisted. "Are *you* Greenscapes, Incorporated? Or is the post of president something of a figurehead?"

His comment nettled her, though Jo admitted there was no real reason why it should. Before she could answer, Alex continued, "Nice strategy, if it is. Very good PR, I'd say."

"Thank you, Mr. Grant, but I'm a little more than a figurehead," she informed him coolly.

"Please, call me Alex," he countered.

"Okay, Alex. Perhaps you'd like to hear the history of the company?"

"Perhaps I would."

"Well, my father founded Greenscapes twenty-five years ago. He started small, but over the years we've gotten to be one of the major foliage design companies in Florida. Not the biggest yet, but we're still growing. My father was in failing health for several years before his death two years ago, so I assumed many responsibilities sooner than I might have under different circumstances. Still, he remained president until he died. Then I took over that spot. We have some very loyal employees, I should add, and an excellent board of directors. My cousin Tim is first vice-president. Currently he's in charge of our newly opened operation in Miami. We have equally competent people in our offices in Tampa, St. Petersburg, Clearwater, Fort Myers and Naples. Except for Miami, we haven't tapped the east coast market yet. But we're having a study done now, and I'm quite sure we'll soon be opening offices in West Palm Beach, Daytona Beach and Jacksonville." She paused for breath, then asked, "Does that answer your question?"

This time around the lopsided smile was wry. Alex nodded, and said quietly, "Yes. And it sets me right in my place, too. I didn't mean my interpretation of your title as a put-down, Jo, though obviously it came across as one. Actually, my comment was intended as a compliment. I thought it was smart business, that's all."

When she didn't reply, Alex went on, "I know what it means to achieve success in today's competitive world. So I'm being sincere when I say I congratulate you. Obviously the reputation of Greenscapes was well known to my company, or we wouldn't have hired you to design the plantscape for the Mimosa Mall. That's why it was such a shock to me when I walked in this morning." He raised a restraining hand as she threatened to interrupt, and added, "Let's not get into that again. What matters now is whether there's time to rectify the situation before the mall's scheduled opening. That's only a week away. If there isn't time, I want to know it now. I'll simply postpone the opening until everything is perfect, but I'll need to have my people send out immediate press releases to keep the public informed. Can you imagine five thousand cars driving around the parking areas in circles looking for an open door when there isn't one?"

"Yes, I can," Jo said seriously. "And we can make your deadline—if you'll get the paint off the roof."

"You're positive about that?"

"I wouldn't say so if I weren't. We'll start tomorrow morning by removing every plant in the mall. It's the planning that takes time. Knowing exactly where all the new plants will go, Mr. Faraday's crew will be able to install them in, say, two or three days. Before they plant again, though, they'll test the soil and make any necessary adjustments based on their findings. As soon as the tests are completed, they'll move fast." Again, Jo paused for breath. "Okay?" she finished.

"How long will the soil tests take?" Alex queried.

"A few hours, at most."

"You're sure?"

"I have a master's degree in plant pathology, Alex," Jo stated. "I can assure you the problem with the plants was lack of light. The soil tests I'm talking about can be done right on the spot. I'm ninety-nine percent certain that they're not really needed, but why take chances?"

"Why, indeed?" Alex agreed. "For my part, I will see that the painters are contacted first thing in the morning, and the skylights restored to their original state as quickly as possible. Craig Franey can coordinate everything."

Jo nodded, then asked, "Suppose when the job's all done you walk in and a beam of sunlight still hits you in the eye?"

"I'll blink and put on my dark glasses," Alex said solemnly. Then he laughed. "Look," he pointed out, "I already admitted that I overreacted. You might have yourself if you'd been expecting a certain ambience, and . . . well, you know the rest."

"You thought you'd be walking into a scene from the *Arabian Nights*, right?"

"Something like that, I guess."

"You'll have it," Jo promised. "Just wait and see." She hesitated, not wanting to pry, then asked, "Do you plan to be here for the opening?"

Alex was looking over the menu, and suggested casually, "How about some nachos?"

"Sounds good."

He beckoned to the waitress and placed the order. Only then did he turn back to Jo to say, "Yes, I plan to be around. I like to attend the openings whenever I can. It gives me a feel for the locale and the residents. When I can't be present myself, I make sure that whoever represents the company reports back to me in detail. Anyway . . ."

"Yes?"

"Well, I'm flying up to New York tomorrow, but I'll only be there a couple of days," he said. "After that, I'm coming back here for a week's vacation. I decided to give myself some bonus time off under the sun. After that, I'll be going to China."

"China?"

He nodded. "Yes, for a consultation concerning a big mall that's planned near Shanghai. I won't be personally involved in the project, but I've been asked to spend a week there in an advisory capacity." He smiled that disarming smile again. "I found it pretty flattering, to tell you the truth. And impossible to be unselfish enough to send someone else from the company to represent me."

"I don't blame you." As Jo digested this latest bit of information, she discovered there were dozens of things she wanted to know about him. She wanted to bridge the gap between the present and those years when he'd been a rock star. She wanted to know why he'd given up his career in entertainment when he'd been such a success. How he had made the transition into planning and building shopping malls all around the globe. What his private life was like. What kind of food he liked. What kind of sports he liked. What kind of hobbies he had, if he had time for such things. Where he lived. What his wife was like. . . .

Jo found herself stuck on that last "what." As she and Alex munched the nachos and chatted about the tremendous growth that was happening all along Florida's "sun coast," the idea of his having a wife became a subject she wasn't ready to broach.

Danforth Alexander Grant, she was discovering, was not only a terrific looking man, he was fun to be with. Jo was astonished at how comfortable she felt with him now, after the bristling impact he'd made only a few hours ago. It was becoming too easy to forget that he was an important client—and she'd learned long ago the folly of mixing business and pleasure. As far as she was concerned, that was lesson one in the textbook on How to Succeed in Business.

Alex Grant, though, was making her feel as if they were out on a first date together. She could readily imagine that he'd called her that afternoon not on a business matter, but because he was a friend of a friend who had suggested he touch bases with her during his Florida holiday. Once in a great while that had actually happened, and she'd agreed to have a drink with a blind date, or go out to dinner. Inevitably, such arrangements were a disappointment. But in this case...well, if Alex were the "friend of a friend" in question, she knew she'd want to see him again.

But Alex would doubtless have the excellent sense to say good-night after a while, and the next time they met would be at the mall opening. Where, she hoped, he'd find himself congratulating her on the marvelous plantscape her firm had recreated. Then he'd be off to China, and that would be that.

She was startled when he suddenly asked, "Would it be possible to tour your nursery when I get back from New York?"

"Of course," Jo answered quickly. "Anytime you wish. Just let me know what's convenient for you."

"Anytime you're free," he said unexpectedly.

Jo assimilated that statement, and decided not to tell him that she seldom took people on tours herself. True, she'd escorted a group only that morning—theater owners who'd come down from Tampa. But during that tour, they'd discussed with her the concept of enhancing their largest cinema complex with a "greenhouse café" where exotic coffees, sandwiches and desserts would be offered to the constant stream of patrons. If the idea took off there, they'd go for it at their three other locations around Tampa Bay.

Normally she delegated tours to members of her staff. Now she justified her intention to escort Alex personally by reminding herself that Danforth A. Grant was a more important client to Greenscapes, Inc. than both the theater owners and the restaurateurs with whom she'd lunched. Malls International was a very big account. It was only natural that the president of the company would expect her to personally conduct him around the extensive nursery grounds.

He went on agreeably, "The tour can be at your convenience, Jo. I plan to keep my time here free as much as possible. I don't snatch a vacation very often, so I want to take full advantage of this opportunity to relax and enjoy. The few times I've been down in connection with the Mimosa Mall project I haven't had the chance to explore this part of Florida. But I did get out to St. Armand's Key and Lido Beach one afternoon last month, and to Siesta Key another time. I really liked Siesta Key. I might even scout around with the thought of buying a place . . . just something small, something purely for escape."

Jo's pulse skipped a beat when she heard that. The thought of Alex becoming a regular visitor to the Gulf Coast was . . . provocative.

"So," he continued, "except for perhaps getting together with a real estate agent and attending the mall opening, I plan to be lazy. Any time you can fit the tour into your schedule will be fine with me." He beckoned for the check, then added with a smile, "I'll be in touch once I'm back."

"Fine," Jo nodded slowly.

Busy with extracting a credit card from his wallet, Alex didn't see her expression. But it struck him that she didn't sound especially enthusiastic at the prospect of showing him around her nursery.

Well, what had he expected? That she'd leap at the chance of seeing him again? He hadn't exactly made the best of first impressions on Josephine Bennett. Of course, she hadn't exactly made a great impression on him, either. But one thing he'd liked about her immediately was that she'd stood up to him. Regardless of the fact that he fell into the valuable client category and she could lose money by alienating him, she'd stood her ground.

Professional integrity had been a lot more important to Jo Bennett than the money. That fact had come across loud and clear, and it was a quality Alex admired very much. He'd had no intention of asking her out for a drink. They could perfectly well have talked in Craig Franey's office. But suddenly he had discovered that he wanted to get to know this intriguing young woman better. He wanted to see her away from the mall, where business was the order of the day.

Well, now he had. And he couldn't remember when he'd felt as relaxed as he had this past hour or so, sitting here with an amber-haired botanist talking about Florida's astounding rate of development, of all things.

Suddenly, the music that had been there all along caught Alex's attention, and he winced as he recognized the melody of a song he'd once sung. Sometimes not being able to sing still hurt. Most of the time, it was a pain he kept locked in the vault of a very distant past.

He glanced up at Jo and had the crazy thought that he'd like to dance with her. He was a good dancer, but most of his ballroom excursions were dutiful performances with the wives of men he dealt with in business. The idea of dancing with Jo, however, was surprisingly stirring.

He asked softly, "Shall we go?" even though he wanted to stay. Of course, he could suggest that they go somewhere else for dinner. Back at the Floridiana by himself, dinner would be a room service affair. He had a dozen long-distance calls to make. Anyway, there was no joy in dining alone in a hotel restaurant. Thinking about that, he wondered how many room service meals he'd had sent up and how many solitary dinners he'd endured by himself in hotels all over the world.

Alex admitted to himself that more often than not he was alone by choice. Wherever he went, he received invitations that many people would have given a lot to accept. But the glamour route had lost its tinsel appeal for him a long, long time ago.

Jo had picked up her purse and was edging out of the booth. Alex knew he'd failed to grab the right second when he might have casually asked her to dinner, and felt totally frustrated as he followed her out of the club. To make matters worse, the clouds that had been looming in the distance all afternoon had now arrived, and a warm tropical shower was drenching everything in sight.

Jo said, "Guess we'll have to make a run for it. Thanks for the drink, Alex. I'll wait to hear from you."

It was not the kind of a farewell Alex wanted from her. And, as he watched her drive away, he wondered what she'd say if she knew he'd had no intention of taking a week's vacation in Florida at this particular time.

The idea had hit him as he'd sat there listening to Jo talk about the colorful keys that formed a natural barrier between the Sarasota-Bradenton mainland and the Gulf of Mexico. She'd been born and raised in Sarasota County, and had the slightest of Southern accents—another intriguing thing about her. But mostly she'd come on as a one-woman chamber of commerce, and she'd done a very convincing job.

He'd barely driven the length of Siesta Key the one time he'd ventured out there when he'd decided it might be nice to buy a small, secluded home on the Intracoastal Waterway with a dock where he could keep a boat. But he hadn't really made up his mind about seriously searching for such a place until just a few minutes ago.

All because of Josephine Bennett?

What was there about her that was so special? He knew many women who were physically more beautiful. His personal address book, in fact, was studded with the phone numbers of raving beauties in at least a dozen different countries, to say nothing of his many acquaintances here in the States. He liked Jo's looks, to be sure. Her dark brown eyes, smooth pink skin, sensuous mouth, striking amber hair. But the special qualities about her went far beneath the surface, he was somehow sure of that. It didn't take much imagination to guess that she must have gone through some pretty rough times with her company, especially after her father had become ill and she'd had to quickly take the helm. She'd obviously weathered those storms. And obviously had guts and a streak of independence a mile wide.

He liked the way she'd handled the whole matter of the wilted greenscape. She'd been more than ready to shoulder a rightful share of the blame, but hadn't minced words when she'd aired her views on painting the skylights—something she plainly considered a stupid move.

Alex grinned into the rainy night. Very few of his business associates would have dared to be as blunt with him as Jo Bennett had been. He hadn't deliberately set out to make himself appear such a tyrant. Actually, his reputation in business was for fairness, above all else. But the people he dealt with usually learned that he drove a hard bargain, brooked no interference, and seldom backtracked... because, more often than not, he was right.

There was no conceit in that personal evaluation. He'd come by his know-how the hard way, by a long period of trial and error.

The lights of the Floridiana loomed up ahead of him. It was a gaudy palace of a place, big and tropical and fun. Alex knew it would appeal to many people, but he'd immediately sensed that Jo wasn't one of them. Nor was it his kind of place, but business was business, and the Floridiana was a terrific investment.

He thought about making reservations somewhere else for the week's vacation he'd suddenly granted himself—a beach bungalow on Siesta Key, perhaps—then decided it would be a waste of time. A woman as attractive as Jo Bennett was bound to have a full social schedule, if and when she took time away from the large company she headed. He couldn't hope to capture enough of her free hours during his holiday week to make the change worthwhile. He'd be lucky if he could latch on to just a few of them!

Alex strode into the hotel, took a private elevator to his penthouse suite, and started making his calls. After spending an hour on the phone, he paused to call room service and ordered a turkey club sandwich and coffee. Then he was back on the phone again, alerting Andy Carson—his second in command—to the fact that he was going to take a week off. The holiday, though brief, would mean a double work load for both men during the two days he intended to spend in New York.

One paid a high price for corporate success, Alex thought ruefully after he and Andy had rung off. He was beginning to wonder if it was really worth the tariff.

Chapter Three

Jo marched into her office the morning after her meeting with Alex Grant and immediately summoned Len Faraday. She seldom issued such imperious commands. But throughout the previous, restless night, she'd been plagued by the suspicion that Len held the key to the greenscape disaster at Mimosa Mall.

When he knocked on her open door a few minutes later, his appearance alarmed her. He looked tired, older, and seemed to have lost weight. It occurred to Jo that she hadn't seen much of Len lately. Their paths didn't cross every day since much of his time was spent in the field, supervising various projects. Even so, they ordinarily met more often than they had of late.

Before she could speak, Len said wearily, "I know why you've called me in, Jo. We heard the news about Mimosa Mall."

Jo was annoyed with herself for not having paused to think that even by this early hour of the morning, Len would already know what had happened. She'd phoned in from her condo before she'd even gotten out of bed, and had left a message on Marge Cassidy's answering machine to the effect that a crew was to be dispatched to the mall right away to begin removing every dying plant.

In issuing that command, she realized now, she'd gone around her most trusted employee. Len was in charge of the project, after all. She should have told him what she wanted done, then let him assign a crew to the job. As it was, she'd caused him to lose face. Still, hadn't he brought this on himself?

Though his appearance worried her, Jo's voice was firm as she demanded, "What happened at Mimosa Mall, Len?"

"Well, number one, I didn't personally inspect the project last week," he confessed. "Naturally I checked with the crew that did the job. Bob Hawley told me that many of the plants didn't look great. He wondered about the water supply, and also decided they needed additional feeding. He mentioned that the atmosphere in the mall was very dry."

"So," Jo said bitterly, "the foliage was overfed and the water wasn't thoroughly tested. Is that it?"

"I'm afraid so," Len admitted. "And...I'm sorry. Sorrier than I can say. I hope you can make the client understand what happened so he'll let us do it right. Believe me, I know how important this project is, and I've been kicking myself for not getting out there the minute Bob spoke to me. The thing is, Bob's never been wrong before."

"Why didn't you go to Mimosa yourself?"

At that, Len Faraday's jaw tightened and his whole body seemed to tense. Looking up, he said, "Jo, about a month ago I discovered I have cancer. Last week I had my first chemo treatment. It made me sicker than a dog, so I mollycoddled myself a little and stayed home."

"My God, Len!" she blurted. "Why didn't you tell me about this?" The problem at Mimosa Mall was forgotten as Jo stared up at the man who'd been a part of Greenscapes, Inc. for so long. This man who'd been a close friend of her father's.

"Because you have enough on your shoulders," Len said simply. "As you've had for a long time. Anyway, the docs tell me we've nicked the demon in the bud. The chemo should do the trick. No surgery indicated right now. A few months, and I'll be as good as new," he finished, forcing a smile.

Jo was literally shaking as she ordered, "Len Faraday, you're going on sick leave as of right this minute!"

Len laughed weakly. "You're a lot like your old man when you talk like that," he told her. "But I'm going to disobey you just as I would have him. There's no way I'm going on sick leave, Jo. That, I don't mind telling you, *would* kill me."

Jo shook her head in disbelief. "That's ridiculous, Len," she chided. "You need complete rest."

"No, I don't."

"Yes, you do."

"Look, Jo, I'll make a bargain with you. I'll take off the day I have a treatment, if I don't feel too good.

Otherwise, you can expect to see me lumbering around here for years to come.''

Len was a widower, and he and his wife had never had children. Jo knew that, but she hadn't realized just how much Greenscapes meant to him until now. Or how terrible he must feel about the fiasco at Mimosa Mall.

''I expect you to lumber around here only when you're feeling one hundred percent well, Mr. Faraday,'' she said thickly.

''How many people do you know who can honestly say they feel one hundred percent, Miss Bennett?'' Len shot back.

''Look, Len, what happened at Mimosa really wasn't Greenscapes' fault.''

''How do you figure that?''

Jo told him about Alex Grant's instructions to have the glass skylights painted in order to diffuse the sunlight. And about how she'd informed Alex that the paint must be removed immediately if he expected Greenscapes to continue handling his account.

When she finished the story, Len laughed. ''I'd love to have seen you doing battle with him,'' he confessed. ''I know some of the men who've been working on construction at Mimosa and believe me, whenever Grant's come around they've quaked. They say he's a devil about perfection, although he's also very fair.''

Even this small bit of information was intriguing to Jo. For all of his fame as an entrepreneur, Danforth A. Grant kept a surprisingly low profile. Otherwise there would have been a lot more about him in magazines and newspapers . . . including stories about his transition from rock star to businessman.

Len Faraday stretched and said, "If you'll excuse me, Jo, I'd like to get over to the mall."

"Look, Len," Jo said, honestly concerned about his health, "there's no need for you to go over there today. Your men can handle the foliage removal. I mean, that's straightforward. What I'd like you to do is check the results of the soil testing. You might also recheck the water the mall is using, to be sure it's as pure as we thought it was. Then, when the new plants are in you might take a look and—"

She broke off, aware of the sardonic gleam in her field boss's eye. "Are you telling me how to do my job?" he queried lightly.

"You know better than that, Len."

For a treacherous moment, his lopsided grin reminded her of Alex. Then he said soberly, "I intend to survive, Jo. So don't waste time worrying about me, okay?"

"Okay," she murmured. "Okay."

With Len gone, she turned to the stack of papers on her desk, a stack that never seemed to diminish no matter how much time she spent on it, no matter how many items she filed. It was, of course, a reminder of how very well Greenscapes, Inc. was doing these days. And Jo was profoundly thankful for that. She only hoped that word of the Mimosa Mall fiasco—a fiasco caused by a comedy of errors—wouldn't cause any harm to the firm's reputation.

"Maybe this'll teach Alex Grant not to be so high-handed," she said aloud. Fortunately there were no

people in the room with her and Marge's computer
printer was clattering away in the outer office.

The day passed. And the next. And the next. Then,
midway through the fourth morning after her meeting with Alex, Marge's voice called through the inter-
com, "It's that man again, Jo."

She needed no further identification.

"I just got in last night," Alex announced. "I suppose you're too tied up to do the nursery tour today?"

She knew she should quickly say, "Yes. I'm sorry,
I am." But couldn't say it. "Well . . ." she tempor-
ized.

"Look, Jo, there's no rush," Alex informed her
pleasantly. "Like I said, I'll fit my schedule to yours.
I don't really have any schedule, I'm happy to say. I'm
free till the mall opens next Tuesday."

"That's terrific, Alex," Jo managed, her heart
pounding.

"Incidentally," he said, "I'm stretching my vacation by a couple of days. I was planning on staying
through the week, and it suddenly occurred to me that
there was no point in returning to New York on Friday."

He spoke as if she were being included in his plans,
and Jo held her breath. She was trying to force herself to concentrate on her prime resolution, "Never
mix business and pleasure." But she failed completely
as she found herself saying, "If you'd like to come
over this afternoon, Alex, I'll have time to show you
through the nursery."

"Have, or make?" he challenged.

She laughed. "Actually, make," she admitted. "But that's only because I reserved today to handle paperwork. It really adds up if I don't stay on top of it."

"Tell me about it," Alex said wryly. "So... what time would be good?"

"Three o'clock?"

"I'll be there," he promised.

Alex arrived at Jo's office five minutes early. By then she was finding it almost impossible to dictate a coherent letter, and knew if she kept on trying she'd only start making mistakes.

When she heard Alex's husky voice in the outer office, her bones turned to jelly. And when Marge came to announce him a moment later, with Alex literally following on her heels, Jo felt as if she were a teenager again, swooning at Danny Forth from the darkened confines of a movie theater.

He looked terrific, but not at all like the staid though handsome businessman she'd confronted at Mimosa Mall just a few days ago. He was wearing a yellow crew shirt open at the throat, comfortable looking khaki slacks and brown leather sandals. He even had the beginnings of a tan, which Jo suspected he'd acquired by the Floridiana's sparkling pool.

He looked relaxed and healthy, even a bit younger. The signs of tension she'd noted the other day had vanished. Jo had heard that really successful people knew how to play as well as work. It was something she'd not yet mastered. Her business, though under better control all the time, still occupied too much of her energy. She'd almost forgotten what it was like to let loose and have fun.

Judging from the way Alex looked, he had learned the secret of balancing both worlds. It was a secret she needed to learn.

Maybe he'll give me lessons! she thought dizzily.

Alex noted the rather dazed expression that flashed across her dark eyes and decided he must have interrupted something. He said quickly, "Look, if you're right in the middle of some heavy concentration, I can wait."

"Not at all," Jo said hastily.

She stood, smoothing down the pleats in her pale blue cotton skirt. With it she was wearing a scooped-neck white blouse and a beautiful handwoven belt in royal blue. It was the fifth outfit she'd tried on that morning, somehow thinking that a meeting with Alex might take place. She'd wanted a casual look, knowing how easy it would be to overdress, and Alex's gray-blue gaze told her she'd made the right choice.

She paused in the outer office to give Marge a few instructions. Marge was happily married and had a couple of teenage kids, but that didn't stop her eyes being highly appreciative as she smiled up at Alex while she listened to her employer.

Alex probably had that effect on most women he met, Jo conceded. And without even trying! How could she ever have thought, the other afternoon at Mimosa Mall, that he had no charisma?

"Why don't we begin the tour right here?" she suggested, steering her mind back on track.

"Fine," Alex agreed.

"So...this farmhouse is where I grew up," Jo began. "After Dad died, I got the idea of converting it into our main office. We were using an old trailer, which was about one tenth of the space we needed. Anyway, I had a couple of walls knocked out, the porch built up, glass sliders put in where the front door was, *et voilà* . . . headquarters!''

"Very nice," Alex said appreciatively. He'd stuck his hands in his pockets and couldn't have looked more at ease. But his keen eyes were taking in every detail of his surroundings and his mind was obviously at work.

Outside, he tailored his long stride to Jo's shorter one as she led him through a series of modern greenhouses. His questions were brief and to the point. Nor was there any doubt about his sincere interest in what he was seeing.

Jo was justifiably proud of the nursery and, as time passed, she relaxed to the point of telling Alex how she felt about the business she'd inherited from her father.

"Dad's concept wasn't incredibly original," she admitted. "He just followed it right through. The bottom line is to bring the beauty of the outdoors inside. Not just pretty arrangements, but functional additions to the home and office that add immeasurably to the atmosphere in which people live, work and relax. Psychological testing has proven that people actually feel better and work better when they're surrounded by live foliage."

"I can believe that." Alex nodded in agreement.

"Surveys show that where a work atmosphere has been embellished with plants, there are actually fewer sick days among employees. The employees are happier and consequently more productive. By the same token, clients who visit offices that have been plantscaped get the favorable kind of first impression that leads to business contracts. That first impression is all-important.''

Jo paused, remembering the first impression that the president of Malls International had had of her work.

"Don't look like that, Jo," he said softly. "The business at Mimosa was my fault, not yours. By tomorrow or the day after, I have no doubt that your plantscape for Mimosa Mall will be good enough to win awards. I could see the potential even when everything was wilting," he added seriously.

"And the skylights?" Jo queried.

"Every last trace of paint should be gone by tonight."

They were walking through an area where specimen trees were being grown in rows. Jo had the crazy feeling that they'd stumbled into a private oasis, though she'd walked down those verdant aisles many times. Later she wondered if it wasn't her flustered psyche that caused her to stumble at that particular moment, rather than an uneven clump of earth underfoot.

It was easy to believe that the stumble was predestined. As was Alex's response. For, as if programmed, his arm shot out to stop Jo's fall, then remained on her shoulder as she turned to look up at him.

They were close, very close. Alone, for the moment, in a rich green world, canopied by a dazzling blue sky. Slowly Alex drew Jo toward him, his eyes darkening as he drank in her nearness. And as that implanted personal warning—business and pleasure don't mix—buzzed in her mind, Jo made the conscious decision to ignore it.

Perhaps it would prove foolish, perhaps insane, but she didn't want to resist Alex. Her upturned face was an open invitation that Alex was only too ready to accept. Very deliberately he took Jo into his arms, then bent his head to claim her mouth with his.

His kiss was velvet. Deep and warm and incredibly stirring. As Jo's senses swam, as those built-in inhibitions began to melt away, she let her surging feelings guide her, let pure instinct replace her usual logic. She knew what she was doing to Alex ... and what he was doing to her. And when he began to draw away, she couldn't bear to let him go. Wordlessly, by the eloquence of her eyes and the urgency of her hands pressing against his shoulders, she invited him back again.

Then ... they heard voices, which was hardly unexpected. A lot of people worked on the nursery grounds, and Jo knew them all. Caution prompted her to step back from her handsome client.

She fumbled with her hair, smoothed her skirt, and confessed shakily, "I don't know what got into me."

"You're not alone," Alex whispered softly. He smiled. "Shall we blame this alluring tropical atmosphere?" he suggested.

"Too many exotic palms?" Jo queried in her turn, striving for a light touch. But there was nothing light about her whirling emotions.

The tour lasted ten more minutes, during which Jo tried to file away the memory of Alex's kiss. Then they went back to her office, and when Alex showed no inclination to rush off, she asked, "Would you like something to drink? Some iced tea, perhaps? Marge keeps a pitcher full out in the kitchen."

"I'd love some," he murmured, settling his long length onto the sofa across from her desk.

As they sipped, Alex posed more questions about Greenscapes, and Jo was glad to answer them. She needed something to get her mind off the impact he was making on her, something to help her keep her feet on the ground.

"Florida's the number one area in the country for foliage production, because of the favorable year-round climate," she told him. "We grow virtually all of the foliage we use in our plantscapes."

"How come I didn't see any flowers?" Alex inquired.

"That's the one area where we buy from others," Jo conceded. "Easter lilies, chrysanthemums, poinsettias, jonquils . . . we buy them from other nurseries as the need arises. Dad and I toyed with the idea of growing flowers, but decided that we'd do better by becoming specialists in one field, rather than by branching out. No pun intended."

Alex laughed. Then he said, "Seriously, I must say I'm impressed. I've known about interior plantscaping since I first started developing malls, but I've never toured a nursery such as yours. A facility, I should say. It's very well organized, which somehow I imagine is your doing."

"Thank you," Jo managed to reply, feeling a slight flush rise to her cheeks. "I minored in business administration, which certainly helped, but . . ."

"But your father taught you the important things," Alex finished for her perceptively.

"Yes, he did."

"What about your mother, Jo?"

"My mother died nine years ago. I was a sophomore in college."

Alex was quiet for a moment. Then he said, "Running Greenscapes demands a constant finger on the pulse, doesn't it?"

"Yes, it does. We're firm believers in TLC for plants, and our maintenance people give them plenty of it. That's why it was so disconcerting to me when I went to your mall the other day."

Alex grimaced. "I really wish you'd get off that topic."

"I can't entirely," Jo confessed. "As a matter of fact, I think it'll loom up to haunt me for a long time to come. But at least I know the reasons why things happened as they did." She hadn't intended to get into the subject of Len Faraday's illness and his consequent failure to supervise the mall job himself. But now she found herself relating it in detail.

Alex listened with a sympathetic ear. When she finished, he said gravely, "One always has to make allowances for the human factor, Jo. Sometimes that's the hardest thing to do. But we all have failings that reflect upon our performance. Sometimes they're avoidable, sometimes not. Frankly, I'd say your Len Faraday is a pretty gutsy guy. I hope you'll set his mind at rest about Mimosa, because the repercussions have already ended. I guarantee I'll give you the highest possible client endorsement."

Jo's eyes widened. "Why should you?" she asked reasonably. "You have no grounds to base any endorsement on yet. Wait till you see what we do at Mimosa this time around, before you commit yourself.''

"There's no need to,'' Alex assured her. "My company checked your local Better Business Council and reported that they've never had a complaint directed their way concerning your company. In twenty-five years, I'd say that's nothing less than incredible.''

"Well, we try,'' Jo said, flushing again.

Alex glanced at his watch. "Whew!'' he exclaimed. "It's almost six. I had no idea it was so late. What happened to this afternoon?'' He grinned at her, then added, "I didn't mean to keep you from your work. And what about your secretary?''

"Marge left quite some time ago. She waved good-bye.''

"Behind my back, eh?''

Alex was staring at his nearly empty glass, and Jo sensed he had something other than Marge's departure on his mind. After a moment, he gazed up into her eyes and asked, "Would there be a chance you might be free to have dinner with me tonight?''

Jo shook her head reluctantly. "Tonight, I can't,'' she said. "I'm sorry.''

"So am I,'' he murmured.

She hesitated, then, not entirely sure of herself, she said, "Actually, I'm going to a birthday party. Maybe you'd like to come with me?''

"Me?'' Alex queried, looking startled.

She laughed. "You might enjoy it. At the very least, you'd see a different side of Florida life.''

"How's that?''

"Well, about a year ago our best designer, Fred Baxter, had a stroke. He's made a remarkable comeback and gets around very well now, though he has to use a cane. He's even doing some free-lance work for us from time to time. When he was beginning to recover, though, he and his wife decided to sell their house. They moved into a mobile home park over on the Manatee River. Anyway, Fred's fifty-two today.''

"That's young to be pushed out of the race," Alex commented reflectively.

"Yes, it was very rough for him. I'm sure it still is. But outwardly, at least, he's adjusted amazingly well. Thanks to his wife Myrna, to a great extent. Myrna's a real jewel. So tonight she's having a surprise party for him. They're holding it in the community center at their park. Myrna's going to get Fred over there with the excuse that she wants to play bingo. Except that there won't be any bingo, of course.''

"Fred doesn't know you'll be coming?''

"He has no idea at all, hopefully," Jo said, shaking her head. "I ordered a cake, which I have to pick up at the supermarket on the way. They stay open fairly late, so there's plenty of time.''

"And you're seriously inviting me to come with you?''

Jo didn't know how to take that. Rather stiffly, she said, "Yes, Alex. My invitation was serious. But I'll understand if you'd rather do something a little more exciting on your vacation than go to a stranger's birthday party. It won't exactly be a scintillating evening." *Just wonderfully warm and very human,* she wanted to add. But she bit back those words.

Looking almost as stern as he had when she'd first met him, Alex said, "Don't misunderstand me, Jo.

I'm not especially interested in scintillating eve-
nings...unless they're shared with someone I truly care
about.''

Someone I truly care about...

The phrase echoed, and Jo felt slightly giddy. She
knew so little about Alex. Nothing about his personal
life, nothing about the women in that life. Nothing
about a lover or a wife.

She was horrified to hear herself ask, "Are you
married, Alex?"

"Married?" he repeated, genuinely taken aback.
"No, I'm not married. Do you think I'd be trying to
date you if I was?" Before she could answer, he went
on smoothly, "I assume the Miss in Miss Bennett isn't
a *mis*nomer?"

"Your assumption is correct," Jo said, trying to
stifle a snicker at his pun.

"Well, what made you think I might be married?"

"You mentioned sharing with someone you truly
cared about."

"There isn't anyone, Jo. Nor has there been, for a
long time," Alex said frankly. "Relationships, yes.
But short-lived ones, due to me, mostly. I guess I'm
not the easiest person in the world to get along with."

He grinned that lopsided grin that made Jo's heart
twist. "For the record," he said, "there was somebody serious, a long time ago. She walked out on me.
It took a while to get over it, but I did. In other words,
there's no broken heart, no unrequited love. I like
women, Jo. But for the past ten years or so I've been
too busy to let anyone into my life on a serious basis."

He paused, then said, "Okay, that's my confession. Now, what about you?"

"Sort of...a parallel story," she said slowly. "Someone a long time ago, yes. I eloped right after high school. His family had it annulled."

"*His* family?"

"That's right. So...it did a job on me at the time. But like you, I got over it." She smiled. "No broken heart," she repeated. "No unrequited love. And I guess I, too, have been too busy to get involved in a serious relationship."

"I'd say that shows where we both stand," Alex mused.

Jo wasn't sure she knew what he meant by that, either. Was he inferring that they were both accustomed to taking pleasure where they found it, without any strings attached? Maybe she'd done that once or twice, Jo conceded, but she already knew, deep down inside, that it wouldn't work with Alex Grant.

If a relationship with Alex ever came crashing down, she'd have a Humpty Dumpty heart and a love so unrequited that nothing would ever make her whole again.

He asked, his voice low, "May I come to Fred's birthday party with you, Jo? That is, if you're sure your friends won't mind having a stranger on the scene."

"They'll love it," she promised.

Even as she spoke, Jo knew that while what she was saying was true, it wasn't the whole truth. Fred and Myrna Baxter would love having Alex at the party, she was certain of that. Alex could only be a welcome addition at any party. But she'd invited him for her own sake, not for theirs, and that might be flirting with emotional disaster.

Business and pleasure, she warned herself. But as she looked up into Alex's handsome face, the warning was lost.

Chapter Four

Jo elected to drive that evening since, as she pointed out to Alex, she knew the way.

They stopped for the birthday cake she'd ordered, then she headed over a cross-country road to Route 41. As usual, this main thoroughfare was choked with traffic.

"Bad hour?" Alex asked sympathetically, after they'd been bogged down for the third time in a line of bumper-to-bumper, barely moving cars.

Jo shook her head. "It's almost always like this," she admitted, "except maybe at three o'clock in the morning. But it's still the most direct route to the Baxters' place."

Alex grinned. "I don't mind in the least being stalled in traffic with you," he teased. "On the other hand, I know it's a pain for the driver. Want me to change places with you for a while?''

"No, I'm okay," Jo said. "Actually, we don't have that much farther to go. We're running a little late, but Marge—my secretary—planned to arrive early and get things organized."

Alex nodded, then asked, with a glance at the highway, "Is this really the famous Tamiami Trail?"

Jo smiled. "Yes. Doesn't look like it sounds, does it? Most people expect a quaint old Spanish cartway. But actually, until the Interstate system came into being a few years back, this was the main road—in fact, the only road—all the way from Tampa to Miami. Hence the name."

"The name's a lot more romantic than the reality," Alex agreed.

Jo smiled ruefully. "That's true of a lot of things, wouldn't you say?"

"Not necessarily," he answered rather enigmatically.

Alex sat back, and Jo stole a glance at him out of the corner of her eye. It was hard to be rational, even to handle the car like the good driver she was, with him so close to her. She'd never before wanted to initiate lovemaking with a man. It wasn't that she was old-fashioned in that respect, rather that she'd never been sufficiently motivated. But it could be quite a different story with Alex.

Wow! Jo exclaimed silently, and quickly threw on some mental brakes.

The mobile home park where the Baxters lived was on the banks of the Manatee River.

"Nice location," Alex commented, as they drove through an entrance flanked by deep pink azaleas in full bloom.

"Yes, I think it's one of the nicest park locations around," Jo agreed. "The Baxters had a fairly large house in Bradenton that they sold after Fred had his stroke. It wasn't an easy thing for them to do because they loved the place. But handling the mobile is so much easier for them, and this park is convenient to the hospital where Fred goes for therapy."

"It may surprise you," Alex admitted, "but I've never been in a trailer. I guess I should say mobile home."

"Most of these places are called mobile homes," Jo told him, "even though they're certainly just about immovable. They're suited to Florida, a lot more so than I imagine they are to most places. The climate and the general atmosphere make them fit in. They've done some pretty nice things with a lot of the parks." She chuckled. "And, of course, most of them are adult communities."

"What's that supposed to mean?"

"Well, you and I couldn't own a mobile home in here if we wanted to," Jo told him, as she slid her car into a parking space outside a long, low, white-painted wooden building. "You have to be at least fifty years old. More often, fifty-five. So we have a way to go...."

She met Alex's eyes as she said that and saw an oddly intent expression. "Yes," he agreed. "We have quite a way to go, Jo."

She tried not to wonder what he meant as she led the way to the community building. Inside Marge Cassidy was lining people up in one corner, and she quickly beckoned Jo and Alex to join the others.

"Here, let me take the cake. I'll stash it in the kitchen. You're just in the nick of time," she told them. "I was beginning to worry that you weren't going to make it. Myrna and Fred should be along any minute."

Jo glanced around, recognizing some of the park tenants. She'd visited Fred here many times before. She nodded and smiled, received nods and smiles in return, and also noted more than a few curious glances in Alex's direction.

Within a few minutes the door to the community building opened and Jo saw Fred, leaning on his cane, with Myrna at his side.

The couple stood there, silhouetted against a golden backdrop. The sun had just set and the glorious afterglow was smudging the western sky with a beautiful blend of colors that merged, one into the other, in a constantly changing celestial pattern.

Jo heard Fred say, "Are you sure they're playing bingo in here tonight, Myrna?"

Then, on cue, everyone shouted, "Happy Birthday!" Overhead lights were turned on, and in their glare Jo saw Fred blink back sudden tears. Since the stroke, he tended to get emotional rather easily. But this was a good, healthy feeling, she reminded herself.

She ran to his side, threw her arms around him, and hugged him fervently. "Happy, happy, happy!" she breathed, her own eyes stinging.

Fred held her close with his good right arm. "Well, Jo, I've made it through another year," he said, in a voice so low only she could hear him.

"And you've got lots and lots of years to go," Jo whispered back, and meant it.

Her eyes still brimming with unshed tears, Jo turned and saw Alex just behind her. He was just the diversion she needed at this choked-up moment. She tugged him forward, introduced him to Fred and Myrna, and then other people began crowding around and she started introducing Alex to them, too.

A number of the women who lived in the park had prepared for the party, and the dishes were set out on a long table covered with a pretty blue paper cloth, around an arrangement of flowers flanked by blue candles in crystal holders.

Guests had a choice of beer, wine, or a nonalcoholic fruit punch. People chatted and joked as they ate and drank, and when she glanced at Fred now and then Jo was reassured to see that he'd got over his earlier emotionalism, and looked as if he was having the time of his life.

Finally the moment came to light the big birthday cake that she'd brought. Fred got to his feet and blew out all the candles at once, causing everyone to exclaim admiringly about his lung power.

Jo helped to serve the cake, putting the slices on blue paper plates. Alex, to her surprise, apparently assumed that he was expected to lend a hand, and began passing the plates around the room. Then, after a time, she saw him draw up a folding chair to Fred's chair, and shortly thereafter she observed the two men in deep conversation. Fred seemed to be completely absorbed in whatever it was they were talking about, and Alex looked equally interested.

The small scene made Jo feel good. It still saddened her to think of Fred's stroke, and the way it had cut short his career. He was such a highly talented man, a natural when it came to designing exquisite plantscapes. She was glad he was once again well enough to do some free-lance work for Greenscapes, and was determined that she'd always find a job for Fred to work on whenever he wanted one.

Now she felt grateful to Alex for giving Fred his special attention. Though people who lived in the park were warmhearted, wonderful and a lot of fun to be with, most of them were considerably older than Fred. They'd been ready to retire. Fred hadn't been.

Since many of the people living in the park were on fixed incomes there was an unspoken rule on occasions like this to keep any gifts limited to "fun" things that cost very little.

Jo had bought Fred a small plastic palm tree that squirted water when its base was pressed. It was one of those tacky souvenirs she usually grimaced at the sight of, but she'd known it would make Fred laugh, and it did.

She was surprised, though, when Alex approached Fred to give him a gift . . . especially since Alex hadn't even known there was any gift-giving involved. Fred displayed it to her proudly.

"It's a casino dollar," he told her. "Alex says he won it playing the slots on the QE II a few months ago. He had to go to England on business, and says he decided to take the ship back and relax a little. Anyway," Fred concluded, "he guarantees this'll bring me good luck."

Touched, Jo smiled and said, "You can bet on that."

"Ouch!" Fred retorted. "That has all the makings of a bad pun."

"Doesn't it, though," Alex said, looming up at Jo's elbow. "I didn't know you were one to make plays on words, Jo."

Fred chuckled. "Never can tell about Jo," he warned Alex. "She's always coming up with something. Trouble is, she never gives you any advance idea what it's going to be."

"Now, Fred . . ." Jo protested.

"It's true," Fred nodded. "She's full of ideas, Alex, this one is. Got more ideas bobbing around in that pretty head of hers at one time than a lot of us have in a lifetime."

"Don't include yourself in that, Fred," Jo told him quickly. "You've got more ideas in your head than anyone I've ever known."

"Used to have," Fred admitted. For a moment he looked a bit misty-eyed. Then he brightened and said, "And, do you know, they're starting to come back again? This silver dollar should give them just the added push they need."

A few minutes later Jo left Alex talking with some of the other men and went out to the kitchen to see if she could help with the cleanup.

The truth was, she needed a little space from Alex for a while. It wasn't that he was overpowering her. But she was overwhelmingly conscious of him. Of his nearness. Of the sight and scent and strength of him.

She didn't have to tell herself that no man in her entire life had ever made the impact on her Alex was making. It was self-evident. And yet she'd seen him on only two days of that entire life. It was crazy, absolutely crazy, to let her emotions become so involved so quickly.

She'd also seen yet another side of Alex tonight, and this particular glimpse was stirring her profoundly. He was coming on as a very warm, compassionate, caring person, ready to give freely of his time and himself. And that was something she hadn't expected.

How many facets were there to Alex? she began to wonder.

She found Marge shooing a number of other women out of the kitchen. "When the time comes to leave you can pick up anything you brought with you," Marge was instructing them. "Aside from that, everything we've used was paper or plastic, and it's all going right into a trash bag."

Having delivered that ultimatum, Marge faced her employer. "Why aren't you back in there with that handsome, handsome client of yours?" Jo's secretary demanded.

Jo had to smile. Marge was such a romantic. She'd married young, and was still totally devoted to Larry, her husband of nearly twenty years. Regardless, Alex's attractions had in no way been lost on her.

Jo said, "I'm giving him a chance to gab a bit with the boys."

"I'd say most of the boys are old enough to be his father," Marge observed.

"Probably. But they've certainly been relating to him."

"So have you, I take it," Marge said softly. Then, before Jo could comment, she added, "Okay, Jo. Don't snap! I'm delighted, you should know that. I can't remember there ever being anyone around who could make you look the way you do right now."

"And what way is that?" Jo asked with mock sternness.

"Beautiful," Marge said simply. And it was the simplicity of the statement that did it. The tears Jo had been holding back all evening filled her eyes.

"Hey!" Marge protested, alarmed. "What's wrong?"

"I'm just sort of...mixed up," Jo confessed. "I admit Alex is very...special, Marge. But I don't even know him."

"Funny," Marge answered, "but I almost have the feeling I do."

"What do you mean?"

"He looks so familiar. He reminds me so much of somebody." Marge paused, frowning. "I would swear I've seen him before."

Alex had become so much *Alex* to Jo that she'd temporarily forgotten all about Danny Forth. Now she felt a pang of apprehension as she heard Marge, because—though she couldn't have said why she felt this way—she had a sudden, overpowering conviction that Alex didn't want to be identified as Danny Forth. Didn't want that other long-ago identity to be revived.

Why?

Jo had no idea. She searched her mind, again wishing that she could recall the memory that would help her begin to update her knowledge of the rock singer who'd played such an important role in her teenage life. The more she thought of it, the more incredible it seemed that someone as famous as Danny Forth had simply... vanished.

Had Danny gotten mixed up in drugs? Or in something so catastrophic that he'd been forced to abandon his career? If he had, Jo felt sure she'd have heard about it, still would have some inkling of it, especially with all the memory nudging she'd been doing these past four days.

"Has Alex Grant ever been around Greenscapes before, to your knowledge?" Marge asked, still frowning. "Maybe when your father was alive?"

"I doubt it," Jo said, and promptly tried to change the subject. Marge needed to be diverted.

"Where's Larry tonight?" she asked.

"Larry?" Marge echoed. "He had to go up to Tampa to get some supplies."

"How's the store going?" Jo persisted. Larry had acquired a franchise from a computer supply house just a few months ago, and was now doing business in a store on the Tamiami Trail.

"The store's doing fine," Marge answered absently, and Jo knew she hadn't diverted her at all. She was vastly relieved when Myrna Baxter came out to the kitchen to say, "Ah, there the two of you are. Jo, Marge, I have to thank you personally for this wonderful party. I haven't seen Fred laugh and smile and joke like this since before he got sick."

Myrna was small and pretty, with prematurely silvered hair. Impulsively she hugged first Jo, then Marge. "The two of you are just great," she said, then added, "As for that handsome date of yours, Jo, he's the best looking thing I've seen in years, and the nicest. Wherever did you find him?''

"He's a client," Jo explained, then changed the subject again, this time to the hospitality of Myrna's neighbors.

Soon they rejoined the others. As they did so, Frank was bemoaning the fact that a lady named Agnes Morrissey was among those missing from the party.

"I was hoping she'd be around to play some piano for us, so we could all sing," Frank admitted.

They discovered that Agnes was in the hospital, though "doing fine," as an elderly man put it. "Her heart's been playing a few tricks on her," he continued, addressing the remark primarily to Alex. Chuckling, he added, "Got to remember that Agnes is pushing eighty, but she thinks she can keep going like she did when she was sixteen."

"Well, more power to her," Alex answered quietly. "I admire people like that. It's easy to keep going when you're in tip-top physical shape. Different and difficult when you're not."

He spoke casually, yet Jo couldn't help but wonder if there was a deeper significance to what he was saying. Had Alex ever had any physical problems? He certainly didn't look as if he had.

She reminded herself that there was a great deal of truth in the old cliché about not being able to tell a book by its cover.

This was demonstrated in quite a different fashion when Alex said unexpectedly, "I can play piano. I'd be glad to bang out some tunes you can sing to, if you like."

Amid a chorus of approvals, Alex moved to the battered old piano in the corner. Someone pulled up a chair for Fred so he could sit down next to Alex and the others gathered around.

He was no virtuoso—his piano playing wasn't at all like his artistry with the guitar had been, Jo thought, watching him and listening to his music. But, as might be expected, he had an infallible sense of rhythm, and she was amused at the old musical chestnuts he was able to recall.

Songs that dated back to the thirties, forties and fifties came alive again under his fingers. Some of them, Jo suspected probably even dated back to the twenties. This was the kind of music these people loved, and pretty soon they were all singing lustily.

Her eyes were on Alex all the time she was singing, and she soon became aware that he wasn't singing at all. She knew that he must be familiar with the lyrics, or at least some of the words to these old popular songs, and wondered why he didn't join in with the rest.

Finally Alex took a break to have a can of beer, but promised laughingly before he left the piano that he'd come back and do another stint before the party broke up. It was then that Jo made her way to his side, saying first, "That was really great, Alex. And great of you to do it."

"It was fun," he said honestly.

"How come you're not joining in the singing?" she asked bluntly, and watched for his reaction.

Alex took another sip of his beer, then said cheerfully, "I can't carry a tune."

He was looking at the beer can as he said it, and Jo was aware he wasn't meeting her eyes. Even so, he spoke so casually that she couldn't say he was being evasive. Had she not known better, she would have sworn that Alex was stating a simple fact.

But she did know better. She knew that he not only could carry a tune but could do virtually anything he wanted with it. When he was at the height of his popularity as a singer, he—Danny Forth, she amended—had sometimes reached back into musical history and ferreted out a song, and then made it his own.

Danny had had a way with songs that made him soar above most rock stars. Part of it was that he'd sung from the heart. Not that other rock stars didn't. But with Danny it had been a special quality—like sharing a God-given gift with the people who were listening to him.

He'd shared music with these people tonight, but in a different way. There had been none of that personal quality, that hard-to-define something that had been so totally Danny Forth. Maybe because his voice had been his instrument, back in the Danny Forth days. Even more so than the guitar that had become so golden and fluent when its strings vibrated under the spell of his racing fingers.

But regardless of anything or everything, why would Alex *lie* about not being able to carry a tune? That bothered Jo, bothered her tremendously, because honesty was the most important thing in the world to her.

She hated liars. She hated everything about lying, even about half truths. Because once you caught a person out in even a half truth you could never fully trust them again. That had happened to her with people she'd cared about, more than once. Inevitably, the relationship—whether with a man she'd fancied herself in love with or a woman she'd thought her friend—had skidded downhill thereafter. Crashed.

She already cared about Alex. Even after spending just a few hours in his company, she cared about him more than she liked to admit. And, since their first, near-catastrophic meeting, everything he'd revealed about himself to her had been increasingly wonderful. She'd liked everything she'd seen, everything she'd heard, everything she'd felt. Until now.

Now, even though admittedly it wasn't a world-shaking issue, she couldn't get his deception—his small deception—out of her mind. She could have understood it if Alex had said he didn't feel like singing. Or if he'd said almost anything . . . except a blatant untruth.

As he'd promised he would, Alex went back for a second performance and, once again, the residents of the mobile home park clustered around him and sang their lungs out. And again his lips didn't move.

Finally Marge said, in mock alarm, "Hey, guys, do you realize what time it is?"

Watches were checked, moans of disbelief echoed. It was well past their usual bedtime for a lot of them. But that obviously didn't matter to anyone. Though Marge's announcement broke up the party, there were smiles on all sides, final birthday wishes to Fred, and an endless string of thank-yous to Alex for having played the piano for them.

Then Jo and Alex were outside together in a night with a tropical moon riding high in the sky, palm fronds blowing gently in the breeze, and the sweet scent of orange blossoms perfuming the air.

It was a night made for love. No doubt about it. Trite though that expression was, Jo thought, as she slid behind the wheel of her car, it was definitely a night made for love.

She glanced across at Alex. He was staring out at the night, looking perplexed.

Suddenly he asked, "Is there something bothering you, Jo?"

They were driving over the bridge across the Manatee River when he posed that question, and Jo had to grip the steering wheel hard to keep from swerving. "Why do you ask?" she hedged.

"Well," Alex said carefully, "I can only say that at some point during the evening the barometric pressure changed between the two of us. I wouldn't be surprised if hurricane-force winds started blowing at any minute."

Jo's mouth tightened. She didn't know what to say to him. Finally she managed, "I'm not much for stirring up storms, Alex."

"Aren't you? What do you do, then? Suppress your anger? That's hard on the blood pressure, Jo."

"No," she said slowly. "I don't suppress my anger unduly. You ought to know that, Alex. I was getting pretty angry at you the other day at Mimosa Mall. And I think it showed."

"Did it ever," he drawled. She glanced at him, saw he was smiling, and she felt . . . terrible. Why had he made that silly remark to her about not being able to carry a tune? Why, damn it?

Jo came very close to asking him. Then couldn't. Because, to tell him she knew very well he could carry a tune a thousand times better than most people would also be to tell him that she knew he'd once been Danny Forth. And she didn't want to do that. What she wished was that a moment would come when he would volunteer that information to her. Part of his life story that he wanted to share with her. Just as there were things in her own life story she would want to share with him.

Into a silence that seemed to be growing thicker and thicker, Alex said, "This is the quietest you've been with me, so I guess I'll do some of the talking. Okay, Jo?"

"Yes?" She held her breath. Was he going to tell her the real reason why he hadn't joined in the singing tonight?

"Well, I want you to know I really enjoyed Fred's birthday party, Jo. And I very much appreciate your taking me with you. It's not often that I have a chance to rub elbows like that with...real people. Great people, all of them. I really liked them.

"Incidentally, I asked Fred if maybe some night he and Myrna could join us for dinner. I thought you might know some place they'd like to go, someplace special?"

Jo wanted to cry, wanted to laugh, wondered if maybe she was pushing herself to the brink of hysteria. She couldn't handle much more of this. Alex's declaration sounded so totally honest, so sincere. But could she believe in it? Could she believe anything he said to her, after that fib tonight? So she just replied, "Sure," and kept her eyes glued to the road.

Temporarily forgetting that Alex had left his car at Greenscapes, she nearly drove him to the Floridiana. In the nick of time she remembered and made the right turns. They arrived at the nursery, which had closed for the night though the extensive grounds were well lighted. She pulled up next to Alex's car, feeling as stiff as a board and knowing she was acting that way.

Alex stood for a moment next to the window on her side of the car, staring down at her through the darkness. His face was in shadows and she couldn't read his expression. Then he bent and swiftly brushed her lips with his. ''Call you tomorrow,'' he promised.

Jo waited till he'd driven off. Then she trailed along behind him until they finally arrived at an intersection where he went one way and she the other.

It wasn't a very good omen.

Chapter Five

Jo usually went to her office on Saturday as though it were any ordinary weekday. She tried to take Sundays off, but didn't always succeed. Sometimes there were conferences with out-of-town clients who couldn't get to Sarasota at any other time. Sometimes she went in for a few hours, just to try to catch up with her endless paperwork.

When she woke up the morning after Fred Baxter's birthday party, though, and realized it was Saturday, she was tempted to play hooky. Marge had Saturdays off, so there would be no one else in the office this morning. Jo did some mental wrestling, remembered the stack of paper she'd left on her desk, and decided to go in, but to go in late. There was something else she wanted to do first.

She detoured on her way to Greenscapes, driving first to Sarasota's modern public library. There she enlisted the help of an assistant librarian and they went through indexes of books and periodicals searching for information about Danny Forth.

There was very little. The most they could find was a couple of articles from old magazines. They profiled Danny at the height of his fame, and said almost nothing about him that Jo didn't already know herself.

Finally the librarian pointed out her need for a specialized reference source if she were to get any real volume of information about the rock singer. But Jo not only didn't have the time to go to such lengths, she honestly didn't want to resort to that much of a search. "Search" was apt to become synonymous with "snoop" and she didn't want to snoop where Alex was concerned. She would much prefer hearing the whole story from him . . . sometime.

As she drove from the library to Las Flores—actually an outlying district of Sarasota that had been real wilderness at the time her father had bought his land there and established Greenscapes—Jo tried to put Alex out of her mind. She needed to direct her attention to some of the other clients she'd be meeting with in the coming week, and to get down all the facts about the varied things they wanted her firm to do for them.

As she turned into the nursery's long driveway, she suddenly felt as if she were seeing Greenscapes for the first time—as if she were viewing it as it must have looked to Alex the other day.

The nursery encompassed several hundred acres. Clark Bennett had bought the acreage in a day when real estate away from the coast or the immediate city environs was cheap. Literally dirt cheap, Jo thought with a slight smile.

On either side of Jo as she drove were acres and acres of plants and trees, as well as row after row of plastic-covered sheds. Closer at hand was the old family homestead she'd converted into an office headquarters.

Jo parked her car, got out, and sniffed. A familiar mixture of aromas filled her nostrils. Basically the smell was of the tropics...moist and warm, laced with the strong penetrating odor of the earth itself, along with an underlying something that smelled like a combination of fertilizer and insect repellant. The smell came from a substance that was used both for plant protection and growth stimulation, as Jo well knew. She'd smelled it all her life.

She detoured again, wandering out toward the shed area, pausing to greet some of the workers and to watch and talk to some of the women she hired specifically to insert the very tiny seedlings into individual peat pots that would later be set in the plastic-covered sheds for further growth. They worked in a permanently roofed-over area, whereas in the sheds the plastic coverings could be drawn back when desired. Primarily the coverings were in place to protect the plants from too much of the hot, Florida sun or, conversely, a sudden cold snap.

As she wandered back to her office, Jo reflected that Greenscapes had come a long, long way since her father had founded it, and people like Len Faraday had come to work for him. Even in the two years since Clark Bennett's death, there'd been a lot of things that would have seemed like real innovations to him. Technology was constantly advancing. And an important part of her work, in Jo's opinion, was to keep up with it. Reading material was always stacked not only in her office, but in her apartment as well. It was impossible to get through all of it before a new batch arrived.

The office seemed very quiet that Saturday. Although there were plenty of people working out on the grounds, Jo was alone in the office building, and she felt the loneliness.

She roamed from room to room, stopping before the computer screen that was linked to their data system so she could instantly obtain information about how much stock was on hand, how much was on order and when certain items were to be shipped. It even showed how much of the various kinds of stock, fertilizers and mixtures was available, and would indicate when further supplies should be ordered.

She wished she could punch some questions into the computer about Danny Forth, and get it to spill out answers.

Unfortunately, nothing involving Alex seemed that simple to her just now.

She tried to settle down at her desk, but was too restless to sit still for very long. Finally she diagnosed her problem. She missed Alex, missed him terribly. And she was beginning to admit to herself that she'd overreacted to his statement about not being able to carry a tune.

She was making a whole range of mountains out of quite a small molehill. It wasn't a deep black lie Alex had told her. If, indeed, it was a lie at all, it was a small white one. Maybe it couldn't even be classified as a lie. Maybe he'd had some simple reason for not joining in, but hadn't wanted to come out and talk about it just then. Maybe he just wasn't one of those people who could do two things at once. Then she thought of him back in the days when he'd played the guitar and sung, and knew she was on the wrong track with that line of reasoning.

She also knew she was rationalizing because she was so attracted to Alex, really liked him so much. Why couldn't she just concentrate on all the good things that had happened with Alex, and let that small fib fade into oblivion?

Because she couldn't. Truth and faith were indissoluble to Jo. Maybe it was a stubborn streak in her nature—she was willing to admit that much—maybe she was too rigid. Even her father had always accused her of seeing everything in shades of black and white. "No grays at all for you, are there, Josephine, my Josephine," he had chided more than once. "Honey, you've got to admit there's a lot of gray in the world."

But the fact was she needed both to believe in Alex and to believe him. And it was rather like poison. A small drop of something bitter and potentially destructive had been introduced into her mind last night, and she couldn't get it out.

On the other hand, he was going to be in Sarasota for only a few days and after that he was going off to China, of all places. Not for long, but she was sure that after China there'd be some other place he'd be traveling to. And when he was based anywhere at all, it was in New York City, a place Jo had visited only once in her life, when her parents had taken her there for a week as a high school graduation present.

They'd made the trek north in July, and though people talked about the heat in Florida in summer, New York had also been stifling, hot, humid, and suffocatingly full of people. She and her parents had done tourist things, like taking a sightseeing bus on which the air-conditioning system had broken down, so that much of the ride had been miserable. She'd been told, since, that to really see and grasp the city one should be with someone who knew it.

Alex would certainly qualify.

For the first time since that postgraduation excursion, Jo wanted to make a return trek to Manhattan, and to find out why so many people seemed to find it the most exciting place on earth.

As it might very well be, if Alex were showing the city to her.

Jo tried again to get back to work. It was nearly noon, and she'd accomplished absolutely nothing. She picked up a stack of papers, determined to go through them one by one.

At that point, the telephone rang.

As he'd preceded Jo out the driveway at Green-scapes the night before, Alex had belatedly realized that he didn't have her home telephone number.

He'd not thought of that as any problem, assuming she would be listed in the phone book. But she wasn't.

She hadn't mentioned whether she worked Saturdays, but he was sure there had to be people around the nursery, just to keep things going. When he called the Greenscapes office at ten o'clock that Saturday morning, though, there was no answer, which didn't exactly advance either his cause or his spirits.

The Floridiana boasted a magnificent pink-tiled swimming pool in the midst of a lavish, tropical garden setting. Alex's bedroom windows looked down on the pool area, and as he watched people splashing around he thought about going down for a swim. His problem was that he wanted Jo to go for a swim with him.

He dialed her office again, and when there was still no answer he started dialing at periodic intervals. Finally he told himself he was being a fool. She probably didn't go into the office at all on Saturdays. Regardless, he kept on dialing.

When, finally, he was rewarded by the sound of her cool, "Hello," he was so startled he didn't immediately answer her.

Again, she said, "Hello?"

Alex found his voice. "Jo?"

"Alex?" He tried to determine whether she sounded pleased or not.

"I wasn't sure you'd be at work today," he said.

"I usually come in on Saturdays," she told him. "Matter of fact, I've only been in the office a few minutes. I was checking around the grounds first. Incidentally, I have a crew over at your mall today. They'll work tomorrow, if necessary, though Len told me he doesn't think it'll be necessary. Most of the plantings are already in place, and he says everything's going to look terrific."

Jo paused for breath, then added, "You might want to drive out that way and see for yourself."

"I don't think so," Alex said quietly.

"Oh," Jo said. It was a small, flat "Oh," but it covered a lot of territory. She realized she'd been babbling but, even more than that, she'd been treating Alex as both client and stranger.

"Jo," Alex said into the silence that hung between them, "I didn't call you up because of anything to do with Mimosa Mall."

"Oh?" Jo said once more, but this time she made it a question.

"I don't have your home phone number," Alex told her.

"Oh?"

"Jo, stop saying that, will you," Alex pleaded, torn between exasperation and laughter. "Look, will you kindly give me your home number right now so I can jot it down."

Jo didn't answer him.

"Jo," he said, proceeding a shade more cautiously, "don't you want me to have your home number?"

"Yes, of course I'll give you my phone number," Jo said, but there was no ringing tone of enthusiastic affirmation to her statement. She rattled off the numbers, and Alex repeated them back, just to make sure he had it right.

"Now," he said. "How much more time do you intend to put in out there?"

"I told you," Jo said. "I just got here a while ago."

"Well, you're not going to stay there all day, are you? Jo, it's terrific out. And this is Saturday...."

"Don't you ever work on Saturdays, Alex?"

Alex almost always worked on Saturdays, at least when he was at headquarters in New York, and his silence gave him away.

"I really do have scads of paperwork I need to catch up on," Jo said vaguely.

"Today?"

When she didn't immediately answer, Alex's perplexity started to grow. Something had happened the previous night, and he had absolutely no idea what it was. One minute, everything had been fantastic between them. Not long after, she'd started looking at him as if he were some kind of a . . . traitor. He'd gone over everything he'd said to the people at the mobile home park again and again. Maybe she hadn't liked it because he'd suggested they have dinner with Fred and his wife one night, though he couldn't see why that could be. Jo seemed to be genuinely fond of Fred. She must realize it would be a treat for Fred to get out to dinner, especially to some place really special.

What had come over Jo? There was a sharp edge to Alex's voice as he said, "Jo, I asked you last night why you were turning off. I'm asking you again now. What did I do?"

He caught Jo off guard. She was admitting to herself that she absolutely yearned to see him again, and that she shouldn't be such a narrow-minded fool. Sometime she'd find out why he'd fibbed to her, sometime he'd tell her. The more she thought about it, the more she was certain of that.

She was trying to think of something he'd like that they could do together. Something outdoors, maybe, where there'd be no chance of too much intimacy. But she wasn't ready to answer Alex's question, and she was a very poor dissembler. Finally she said, "Honestly, Alex, it's nothing." Which, after all, was pretty much the truth, when she got right down to it.

Unfortunately, she waited too long to speak. It irked him that she wouldn't level with him, and his voice sounded harsh as he said, "I was going to suggest you come over to the Floridiana for a swim. But I can appreciate that you're probably anxious about getting caught up with your paperwork." He tried then to temper his sarcasm. "I know the feeling," he added.

Jo caught the frost in his voice and inwardly winced. This wasn't what she wanted at all but, she reminded herself, she had only herself to blame.

"Alex," she began.

"Yes?"

"Look, I thought maybe you might like to drive down the line a way, perhaps see some of the other beaches. You mentioned you liked Siesta Key?"

"Yes."

"Have you been down to Casey Key?"

"No."

"There's a good seafood restaurant near there, with a nice view of the Intracoastal. Would that appeal to you?"

"Are you thinking of lunch or dinner?"

"I was thinking of a latish lunch, to tell you the truth," Jo said, beginning to feel somewhat encouraged because he hadn't immediately vetoed her suggestion. "I skipped breakfast this morning and the hunger pangs are setting in."

"Okay. Shall I pick you up at your office?"

"No," she decided quickly. "This is out of the way for you. Why don't I pick you up at the Floridiana?"

"Okay. When?"

She glanced at her clock. It was just about noon. "How about one o'clock?" she suggested.

"I'll be waiting out front," Alex told her, and after they'd hung up she thought *that* over. Was he inferring that he didn't want her in his room? Was he suddenly drawing back, getting cautious? Had he come to the conclusion they'd gotten into too much, too soon with each other? Was he about to resume a client relationship with her? Oh, she wanted Malls International Ltd. as a client, all right. But she wanted something else entirely from Alex Grant.

As she drove toward the Floridiana to keep her appointment with Alex, Jo was again reminded of her father's admonition about being able to see only black and white.

From now on, I'm going to start studying shades of gray, she promised herself. And could imagine how her father would have chuckled disbelievingly.

Alex was standing in the shade of the hotel's marquee. He quickly came over to the curb when Jo pulled up. As he got into her car, he observed, "You do seem to be the one who draws the chauffeur duty."

"Glad to oblige," Jo said, with a mock salute. She smiled, but the smile didn't entirely reach her eyes. Fortunately they were obscured by the dark prescription glasses she used for daylight driving. Fortunately, because she'd come to realize that Alex was one of the most discerning individuals she'd ever met. And she suspected he'd already begun to read her like a book.

He, too, was wearing dark glasses. And light gray slacks. And a white, open-throated sport shirt. He looked fantastic. She would have sworn he was even better looking today than he'd been yesterday.

"Did you get in a swim?" she asked, primarily to start conversation.

"No," he said. And added, "I settled for a cold shower."

Jo could have used a cold shower herself. Just being next to Alex Grant was . . . doing things to her. Stirring her up, making her intensely aware of her body, every blasted pore and atom of it.

She thought about the previous night again and said, "Alex, I know I mentioned it. But thanks again for being so great to Fred and Myrna and all the rest of those people. It was very kind of you."

"Damn it, Jo," he said, his irritation showing, "I wasn't being kind. I enjoyed myself. I enjoyed myself very much. It was a privilege to be there."

She glanced at him suspiciously and would have sworn he was sincere, though she found it nothing short of amazing that a wealthy, successful, still-young entrepreneur like Alex Grant could find attending a sick man's birthday party in a mobile home park a privilege. Alex, with his looks, money and connections, would be more than welcome in any society he chose to frequent. He probably could become an international playboy, if he chose that route.

Honesty forced her to admit she couldn't imagine him choosing it.

She asked suddenly, "Where do you live, Alex?"

"Huh?" he asked, startled.

"Where do you live?"

"What do you mean?"

"You do have a place you call home, don't you?" she asked impatiently.

"Well, I guess I call Manhattan home, as much as any place. I do a lot of traveling."

"Well, then, where do you live when you're in Manhattan?"

"I own a condo on Beekman Place, overlooking the East River," he said somewhat shortly. "Why?"

"Just wondered. Do you entertain a lot?"

"Business entertaining, but then I have it catered, usually at a hotel."

"Don't you like to entertain at home? Aren't you a secret gourmet chef, or anything like that?"

"No. As a matter of fact I'm a lousy cook. It's something I never got into. Maybe I'd like it if I did. I don't know. There's never been much time or any real chance for hobbies like that."

"What sort of hobbies do you have?"

"I eat amber-haired girls," Alex said calmly.

Her attention veered away from the road long enough to gape at him. *"What?"*

He laughed. "Well, you asked for it," he told her. "What was that? A basic questionnaire for some specific purpose, or is there a chance maybe you're drumming up a little interest in me, after all?"

Jo knew her cheeks were flushed; she could feel them burning. Slowly she said, "I'm sorry."

"Why should you be sorry?" Alex inquired amiably.

"I don't know what prompted me to start throwing out questions like that. I guess that, well, that you tend to come on as something of an enigma, and I, well, I guess I wished I knew more about you, that's all.''

"I'm flattered," Alex said smoothly. But, Jo noted, he made no offer to tell her the story of his life.

Why? she asked herself again. Why was he so reluctant to open up about the past? Was he *ashamed* of once having been Danny Forth? What kind of an "end" had her teenage idol come to?

Jo and Alex lunched in the restaurant near Casey Key that she'd told him about. They sat at a window table overlooking the Intracoastal Waterway, which in this section was studded with mangrove islands.

There was a constant procession of boats, most of them small cabin cruisers, fishing boats or an occasional sloop. Jo wanted to ask Alex if he liked fishing or boating. If he owned a boat. But she was determined not to put any more questions.

So, apparently, was he. They centered their conversation on safe topics like Florida's weather, the threat of hurricanes several months of the year, the fact that tornadoes hit the area every now and then. Jo asked Alex if he'd yet been out to Myakka River State Park, only a few miles inland. There you could take a boat ride with an operator who usually managed to arouse a satisfactory number of alligators for the on-board tourists. Alex hadn't been to Myakka. He seemed interested, but not overly so. Jo filed away the thought that they might take a picnic out to the park one day.

As the time passed, what really began to bother her was that Alex was being so polite and noncommittal with her. She had the uncomfortable feeling that she'd blown something with him. Probably because she'd

evaded telling him what it was that had bothered her.
Well, damn it, he had no cause to complain. She'd
caught him in a downright lie. . . .

She sighed. There it was again. No grays. Black and
white. A character trait, she thought unhappily. She
was probably too honest for her own good.

Lunch finished, she drove over the creaky little
bridge onto Casey Key, then went the length of the
key. It was a drive that always fascinated her. Lushly
tropical, this route made one at the same time keenly
aware of how fragile the barrier islands off the Florida coast really were, some more so than others. On
Casey, the Gulf encroached to the west. The Inland
Waterway wasn't all that far away to the east. In between, houses and vegetation maintained a tenuous
hold that could easily be swept away by even a single,
major storm. Jo didn't want to think about the potential involved in a real unleashing of nature's fury.
Everything about life—and nature—was totally un-
predictable, after all. This was just a more than usually graphic demonstration.

Under other circumstances, she would have been
sharing some of these thoughts and theories that were
close to her heart with Alex. But he'd become even
more remote, maintaining that same, hard-to-assault
politeness as they paused at the beautiful beach at
Nokomis to get out and stroll along the sand for a
while.

"Along here, especially at Venice, a little farther
south, you can still find fossilized sharks' teeth," Jo
ventured, as they walked side by side.

She was so painfully aware of his height, his physique, the sheer force of his close physical presence.

She wanted to reach out and wind her arms around him. Play female boa constrictor. *What an awful comparison,* she told herself. Nevertheless, it was true. She wanted to wind herself around Alex, to bring him close—emotionally as well as physically.

He murmured, "Fossilized sharks' teeth, eh? Interesting."

Jo fought an impulse to shove him toward the light green waters of the Gulf. "They make necklaces and things out of them," she said feebly. "They're millions of years old. Sometimes people find fossilized whales' teeth, too."

"Do the whales' teeth make even better necklaces?" he inquired politely.

"Alex!" She could stand it no longer. "Will you come off it?" she snapped.

"Ah, well," he said, with an infuriating grin. "So, maybe I still can get a rise out of you."

He touched her bare elbow with his finger and rubbed it experimentally over her flesh. That was all it took to send Jo's senses spiraling. She marveled how a man could arouse a woman by merely touching her elbow with his finger.

Alex could.

There were quite a few people on the beach. Otherwise Jo felt reasonably sure she would have pulled Alex down onto the sand, rolled all over him....

She caught her breath. Never in her life had she thought such thoughts.

Alex didn't pursue things. He picked up a shell or two and after a time they switched directions and went back to the car.

He kept the same, light note between them as she drove him back to the Floridiana. He didn't ask her to come in, nor even mention the fact that tomorrow was Sunday and perhaps they could do something. Go out to Myakka and flush alligators? Or . . . something?

As she drove away from the Floridiana, heading for the emptiness of her own condo on the bay, Jo was thinking unhappily that she'd surely managed to turn him off. The problem was, the same kind of electrical disconnection wasn't working for her.

Chapter Six

The opening of the Mimosa Mall was scheduled for ten o'clock Tuesday morning.

Late Monday night, Jo and Len Faraday drove over to the mall together to be sure that everything about the plantscape was right.

As she stood by Len's side, surveying the work that had been redone, Jo knew that no matter who had done this job it couldn't possibly be more beautiful.

The Arabian Nights atmosphere had been fully captured. There was enchantment at every turning, oasis after oasis where weary travelers could rest. Lushness, gorgeous foliage with rich green leaves, exotic flowers, perfection.

Jo turned to Len, her eyes shining. "You've done it!" she said proudly.

"It should have been like this the first time Mr. Grant saw it," Len mumbled.

"Some things are better the second time around," Jo answered back.

But her cheerfulness disappeared once she and Len had parted company and she'd driven back to her condo. She was, of course, going to attend the mall opening. She'd received a special invitation, encrusted with a small gold Aladdin's lamp, the mall's insignia. She knew Alex would be at the opening, too. But she hadn't seen or heard from him since late Saturday afternoon when she'd dropped him off at the Floridiana.

Sunday she'd lounged around her apartment, keeping one ear cocked for the phone. Finally she'd plunged into cleaning out a closet that didn't need cleaning, going through her costume jewelry and arranging it according to colors, straightening up the cabinets in her small kitchen, and doing an assortment of other things all of which, she knew, came under the heading of making useless work.

The telephone remained mute.

Monday, Jo went to work earlier than usual because she'd developed a bad case of cabin fever and had to get out of the condo. Fortunately, Monday was a very busy day. It was late when she left Greenscapes. She was slightly hungry but didn't want to bother fixing food for herself, so she pulled into a drive-in and had a hamburger and some iced tea served to her in her car.

It was a warm night. Sultry. Jo hoped the morning wouldn't bring thunderstorms, literally putting a damper on Mimosa Mall's opening.

It didn't. Tuesday was a perfect day.

The official ceremonies took place in a lovely patio area on the mall grounds. Folding chairs had been set up for invited guests, and there was plenty of standing room for the curious. Alex had vetoed an ordinary ribbon-cutting ceremony, stating that he wanted something a bit more special.

Jo's ticket entitled her to a seat in the reserved section. She took it, trying not to look around for Alex too obviously. Finally, he appeared out of nowhere and strode toward a small podium that was flanked by masses of colorful hibiscus.

He was wearing a white suit and a deep green shirt. To Jo he looked incredible. And he certainly showed no evidence of having lost any sleep Saturday, Sunday or Monday nights. She, on the other hand, had tossed and turned on all three occasions, and had dark circles under her eyes to show for it.

Alex made a short speech about Mimosa Mall that set exactly the right tone. Jo knew his talk was being broadcast throughout the entire outdoor area so that all the people clustered at the mall entrances, waiting for the doors to open, would hear him.

He'd geared his talk in fact to those people, rather than to the various dignitaries—including the mayor and other officials—who were seated in the reserved area. He stated emphatically that he wanted this to be *their* mall, a place where they could come to rest and refresh their spirits as well as to shop.

"And," he concluded, "I think you're going to find you can do exactly that, thanks to the efforts of Miss Josephine Bennett, Len Faraday and the other people at Greenscapes, Inc., who've made Mimosa Mall into the most beautiful oasis possible. *Your* oasis."

On that word, thousands of pink and turquoise balloons were released to soar skyward over Sarasota and Bradenton.

"Each balloon," Alex said, picking up the mike again and speaking above the cries of surprise and delight, "bears Mimosa Mall's logo—Aladdin's lamp. And you'll find each balloon inscribed, as well, with the mall's theme, 'The shopping oasis where you can turn your fantasies into reality.' That's the way we want Mimosa Mall—to be exactly what you want it to be."

"Also, you'll find a gift certificate tucked inside each balloon . . . so watch for them when they come to earth."

"In addition," Alex continued, "the first five thousand visitors to the mall will be given small golden replicas of Aladdin's lamp, emblazoned with our slogan." Alex laughed. "Rub your lamp, and who knows what genie may appear!"

He stepped down from the podium to a burst of applause and laughter.

Jo was watching the balloons filling the sky over her head. Then, as if something were tugging at her, she lowered her eyes and saw Alex shouldering his way toward her through the crowd.

He favored her with his charismatic, lopsided grin. "Corny, I admit," he said, glancing upward at the balloons while speaking in a tone so low that only she could hear his words. "But effective, don't you think?"

"Oh, yes," Jo agreed. "Mimosa Mall will definitely be on the map by nightfall, when hundreds of lucky people find your balloons drifting around their backyards."

He eyed her suspiciously. "Do I detect a note of cynicism in that statement?"

"No," Jo said sincerely. "I meant it. It's a very good promotion."

"Hmm," Alex said, and seemed about to say something more. Instead, he regarded her levelly for a long moment, the smile wiped off his face. Still looking very serious, he asked, "May I drive you to the luncheon, Jo? I'd like it if you went with me."

It was Jo's turn to be hesitant. She'd been invited to the luncheon, which was scheduled to follow the opening ceremony. Earlier she'd thought of going. But after living through the past two bleak days, she'd decided against it.

She'd felt it necessary to attend the mall opening, and had driven over with Len Faraday. Len had not been invited to the luncheon, and discovering that had reinforced Jo's decision not to go herself. With Len by her side, she might have been able to get through it. As it was . . .

She said slowly, "I'm not going to the luncheon, Alex," and was surprised at the look of intense disappointment that crossed his face.

Why, she asked herself irritably, should he be disappointed? He'd virtually brushed her off when she'd driven him back to the Floridiana Saturday afternoon. She'd heard nothing from him all day Sunday, all day Monday. . . .

"Can't I persuade you to change your mind, Jo?" he asked softly. "Look, I know we've lost the beat somehow...."

It was the first potentially musical allusion she'd ever heard him make and Jo raised her eyes to meet his. She was surprised at the unhappiness she saw reflected. "Jo," Alex said quietly, "we need to talk."

There were people standing around in clusters, glancing in their direction, making Jo self-conscious. Obviously these people wanted to speak with Alex— the mayor among them.

"Look," she said, "your public awaits you, Alex. Why don't you call me later?"

"Because I'm not even sure you'll answer the phone," he stated stubbornly.

"Alex, please. Honestly, if you'll just glance over your shoulder you'll see there are people waiting to congratulate you. You should be getting on to the luncheon, anyway."

"If you don't come with me," Alex muttered, "I'm going to skip out on the damned luncheon myself."

"Alex, that's ridiculous," she protested. "Childish."

"Maybe. A man has a right to be a little childish now and then."

"Alex, people are *looking* at us," Jo implored. She was growing more and more uncomfortable.

"Come with me, Jo. We can decide afterward where to go, what to do."

She sighed, then decided the easiest course was to yield.

"Okay," she said. "But I have to go find Len and tell him I won't be driving back to Greenscapes with him."

"I'll wait for you," Alex promised, and finally turned his attention to the mayor and the others.

It wasn't until they reached the restaurant that Jo realized the luncheon was going to be quite a big affair. Cars were being valet-parked. People were milling all over the place. Most of them evidently wanted to shake Alex's hand and congratulate him on Mimosa Mall.

In the throng Jo became separated from Alex. Inevitably, she thought wryly, unless she'd actually clutched his arm and then clung to it. She went ahead toward the dining room, expecting that he'd catch up with her. After handing her invitation to the head waiter, she was led to a table.

It wasn't until she was seated and the room was rapidly filling up that Jo saw that she and Alex were not about to have lunch "together". Alex was shepherded toward a long banquet table and seated in the midst of a number of dignitaries.

Jo saw him glancing around impatiently. He looked like a thundercloud. Within seconds he spotted her. She saw him start to his feet and she violently shook her head. She didn't want to be embarrassed by having Alex take her up to the head table and make her share the limelight with him.

Alex got her message and relapsed into a scowling silence. It was a moment before he rallied enough to bestow a smile upon the woman sitting next to him at the table, this evidently in answer to a question he'd been asked—a woman at least old enough to be his mother, Jo saw with satisfaction.

Jo never did know what she ate at that luncheon. Nor what she said to her table companions. A conversation was carried on in which she dutifully took part. But all the while she was thinking about Alex and trying to figure him out.

Why would he be so upset about her saying she didn't plan to attend the luncheon, when he hadn't even bothered to get in touch with her since Saturday afternoon? He had given her the impression he'd written her off. Why?

Whole armies of "Whys" raced through Jo's bewildered head, and she realized that one of her problems was that she hadn't had any decent sleep for three nights. She never had been able to think clearly on insufficient sleep.

As dessert was being served, Jo mumbled a few words to her table companions, then got up and headed for the rest room. She felt as though she were coming down with a fever. After splashing cold water on her face again and again, she refreshed her makeup, then took a few moments to compose herself.

Alex was waiting for her right outside the rest room door.

He looked grim. There was no other word for it. He looked very grim. And she saw lines of fatigue in his face that hadn't been evident out in the bright sunshine of the mall's patio. Hadn't he been sleeping well either, after all?

He reached for Jo's arm before he said anything, and held on as if making certain she wasn't going to slip away from him again.

"Let's cut out," he suggested abruptly.

"Alex, you can't," Jo protested.

"The hell I can't," he retorted, looking even grimmer.

"Look," he added, after watching her go through a long, moment of indecision, "I already let Andy Carson know I was going to try for the big escape."

"Andy Carson?"

"My right-hand man. I didn't get a chance to introduce you to him at the opening. He's the one who's sitting on the other side of the mayor."

Alex looked at her, narrowing his eyes slightly. "Anyway..." he started. Then he shrugged. "Okay, if you don't want to come along with me, just say so," he stated abruptly.

"I'll come," Jo decided.

They made their way out of the restaurant and across the parking lot. Jo began to feel like a kid playing hooky from school. Alex started up the car and asked, "Anyplace in particular you'd like to head for?"

"No."

"Okay. Then let's try out the beach first."

By "the beach," Jo discovered, he meant Siesta Beach.

She prayed, as Alex pulled into the huge public lot, that he wouldn't be frustrated by failure to find a place to park. Siesta Beach had the reputation of being one of the most beautiful beaches in the world, and it was enormously popular. On a height-of-the season March afternoon like this, parking spaces were sometimes impossible to come by.

Alex lucked out. He slid into a space between a red Corvette and a camper. "Want to walk?" he asked Jo.

"Yes," she replied.

They were both wearing dark glasses. Jo wondered if she looked as inscrutable to Alex as he did to her. She kicked off her slim white pumps and left them in the car, then followed Alex up to the wooden boardwalk.

In silence they crossed over to the sand and walked until they reached the tide line. On this stretch of the beach the sand was hard-packed and remarkably cool, despite the blazing sun.

They walked in one direction for a long time, turned by mutual accord, then started back the way they'd come. Jo detoured to wade in the shallow waters. For a moment Alex stood watching her, and she would have given a mint to be able to read his mind. Then he joined her.

They splashed along without saying anything. But some of the tenseness Jo had been feeling since Fred's birthday party began to dissipate. After a time, Alex reached out a hand. Jo didn't need a second invitation to grasp it.

Slowly they made their way back to the car. Then, settled behind the steering wheel, Alex looked across at Jo. "Got any plans for the rest of today?"

"I intended to go back to work, that's all."

"That's all?"

"Yes."

"Does that mean you could be persuaded not to go back to work?"

She smiled impishly. "I think maybe I could be. I'll have to call Marge and tell her."

"Come back to the Floridiana with me, will you?" Alex urged. "I know it's not your kind of place, but if you'll let yourself go and pretend you've been re-born into the nineteen-twenties I think you'll have fun. We can languish around the pool and pretend we're decadent."

Jo laughed. "Doesn't sound too bad," she allowed, knowing that not much Alex might suggest to her could sound anything but good. "But I'll have to stop by my place and pick up a bathing suit. It's just a short drive from the Floridiana."

"No problem," Alex assured her.

They pulled up in front of Jo's condo and she hesitated only briefly. "Want to come up?" she asked Alex, and at once her pulse began skipping around.

"Thanks, I'll pass this time," he said, and Jo didn't know whether to be glad or sorry.

In her apartment, Jo first placed a call to Marge, who was so delighted to think her boss was going to take the afternoon off and go swimming with Alex Grant that it was almost embarrassing. Then she pulled out all her bathing suits, spread them on the bed, and tried to come to a sensible decision about which one she should take with her to the Floridiana.

The white bikini was definitely too revealing. So, in its way, was the yellow maillot. Finally Jo settled for a slim, bronze, beautifully made suit, and only when she was on her way back downstairs realized that it probably was the most seductive one of the lot.

Alex's suite at the Floridiana was actually bigger than Jo's condo. He thoughtfully turned over his bedroom and adjoining bath to her and changed, himself, in a small powder room off the living room.

They met in the center of the living room. Alex was wearing a pair of dark red bathing trunks that looked as if they'd been designed for him alone, and left little to the imagination. He was a fantastic physical specimen, Jo thought a bit dazedly.

He had thrown a towel over his shoulders that did nothing at all to detract from the picture of his golden tan, well developed muscles... and other masculine attributes.

Jo was wearing a chocolate-brown terry robe, belted at the waist. It wasn't until they'd selected a couple of chairs by the pool and she slipped off the robe that Alex got a good look at her. He couldn't suppress a low whistle.

Jo shook her head disapprovingly. "Honestly, Alex," she protested as she stretched out and began rubbing sun screen on her legs.

"Honestly, yourself," Alex rejoined briefly. "If you'll excuse me, I think I'd better jump in the deep end and cool off."

Jo watched him dive, watched his long, sure strokes as he cleaved expertly through the water. Longing twisted inside her. She knew it would take more than a "jump in the deep end" to cool her off where Alex was concerned. This kind of wanting was new to her and different. Though she'd always considered herself pretty normal where men were concerned, she'd always had a lot of self-control. She still liked to think that she had a lot. But she didn't want to delude herself. Proximity to Alex was tremendously exciting...but dangerous. *You'd be an idiot to forget that,* Jo warned herself.

Alex came back to her, dripping wet, his dark hair sleeked back. "Hey!" he protested. "I thought you were going to join me."

"After a while," Jo hedged, pretending a laziness she didn't feel.

Alex stretched out on the deck chair next to hers. She swallowed hard as she got a good, full view of him. "Want some of my sun lotion?" she asked hastily.

"I don't think so, thanks," he said. "I've got a pretty good head start on a tan. Anyway, it's past midafternoon," he added. "One doesn't burn as easily this time of day."

Jo nodded agreement. She closed her eyes, and felt, rather than saw, Alex stir at her side. Finally she sneaked a look at him behind the camouflage of her dark glasses. He'd flipped over onto his stomach. She saw a broad back, slim waist, tapered hips. Strong legs sprinkled with tendrils of dark hair.

"You analyzing me again?" Alex asked.

She was startled. "What?" Then, reproachfully, "Do you have eyes in the back of your head?"

He turned over, propped himself up on an elbow and looked down into her face. "I don't have to see you. I can *feel* it when you're looking at me," he informed her. "Jo..."

"Yes?"

"Jo, do you know it's just a week ago we met?"

She'd been thinking about that at regular intervals. "Yes," she said.

"Sometimes I feel like it was three seconds ago. Sometimes I feel like I've known you through all the centuries since the world began. Things are happening to me I don't fully understand," Alex confessed. He went on with a smile, "How could a little girl like you sweep me off my feet?"

That brought Jo to her feet. "Little, yourself!" she retorted. "I'll race you to the pool."

She got to the edge first and dived in. Within seconds, Alex caught up with her. There were a lot of people around the pool area, but there weren't that many in the pool itself. Alex grabbed her and suddenly pulled her down until they were both under water. Then, while she was still off guard, she felt his lips pressing on hers. The water was cool, but his lips felt scorching hot. The result was incredibly heady.

He let her go. She pushed her way to the surface and stuck her head above the water, sputtering. He was at her side, treading water. "Okay?" he asked.

By way of answer, Jo suddenly grabbed his shoulders and pushed him under. This time it was her turn to be aggressive. She branded his mouth with her kiss then quickly swam away from him, finally coming to the surface near the shallow end of the pool.

It was inevitable that he challenge her to a race. But it was a shock to his ego, she saw to her delight, when she won despite his greater power and longer strokes.

He pulled himself up to the pool edge and sat looking down at her as if he couldn't believe what had just happened. "For such a little thing . . ." he began teasingly.

"Come back here in the water and say that again!" Jo challenged.

"And just what to you plan to do to me, Miss Bennett?" There was laughter in Alex's husky voice…and a considerable challenge of his own as well.

He let her off the hook before she was forced to answer. "Where did you learn to swim like that?" he asked her.

"I'm a Floridian," she reminded him. "I was practically brought up in the water."

"I should have remembered that," Alex muttered.

Jo was holding on to the edge of the pool, treading water as she looked up at him. "Where did you grow up, Alex?" she asked him.

It was an unplanned question. She hadn't intended to try to get personal with him again. Not until things had eased some more between them, until she'd given him enough room to start telling her about himself without her prompting.

She saw his expression change. He kept on smiling, but it was not quite the same smile. There was a wariness about his eyes and in the set of his mouth. "Oh," he said, "I grew up here and there. Never got a chance to swim twelve months of the year, though."

He changed the subject. "How about coming back on dry land and going over to the pool bar for a drink?" he suggested.

"A couple more laps and I'll do that," Jo promised.

She needed the exertion of swimming to get a grip on herself. Alex's reluctance to tell her about Danny Forth was bothering her more and more.

As she went back to her deck chair, dried off, and slipped on the terry robe, she wondered if anyone else had ever identified Alex.

The chances were that a lot of the people he dealt with in corporate business never had been big rock fans. Or if they had been, they just had never made the connection. After all, Danforth A. Grant looked very little like Danny Forth unless one actually searched for similarities. Even Marge, who'd evidently been something of a Danny Forth fan, still hadn't been able to pinpoint the reason why Alex looked so familiar to her.

It would take a real aficionado like herself to identify him quickly, Jo concluded. Evidently Alex hadn't come across many, if any of those real fans in recent years. He traveled in different circles, felt safe. Although she still couldn't understand why he needed to feel safe.

She strolled by his side to the thatched-roof pool bar. They perched on high stools and ordered strawberry daiquiris. A reggae band began to play, and the tropical tempo was a blood-stirrer in itself. Not that Jo needed anything to stir up her blood, with Alex sitting right next to her.

They began to talk a bit about the mall opening, and how well it had gone. Jo told Alex she wanted one of the small gold Aladdin lamps he'd been giving out for her very own. He promised she'd have one. She thanked him for sending Len Faraday a special invitation to the opening. "It meant a lot to Len. He felt terrible about that whole fiasco," she said.

"Well, he has nothing to feel terrible about now," Alex assured her. "The plantscape couldn't be more beautiful."

They decided on a second round of daiquiris. They were facing west, and the sun was starting its descent. Molten gold poured over everything, anointing Alex in the process and converting him into a bronzed, modern Adonis.

As the sun continued toward its flaming rendez-vous with the horizon and the other side of the world, Jo's desire for Alex began to flame toward the edge of control . . . and when he spoke her name huskily she knew he felt the same way. And that they both wanted the same thing. Each other.

They were silent on their way up in the elevator to his penthouse suite. Still silent, he took out the key he'd put into a small pocket of his bathing trunks and opened the door.

"Well," a masculine voice greeted them. "I was wondering if you were going to get back before I have to head for the airport and catch my plane."

Andy Carson—whom Jo recognized from having seen him at both the mall opening and the lun-cheon—sauntered forth to meet them, a Scotch and soda in hand.

Maybe it was a reprieve, Jo tried to tell herself, as she dressed in Alex's bedroom. Maybe it was better for both their sakes that she and Alex had been inter-rupted.

But she couldn't bring herself to really believe that. As she combed her hair and then put on some lipstick and a trace of eye shadow, she had to admit that Andy Carson's sense of timing couldn't have been worse.

Alex had introduced them. Andy had reminded her that he'd met with her cousin on his last visit to Sara-sota, since she'd been away at the time, and was de-lighted to have the chance at last to meet her personally. He'd pleasantly explained that he had his own key to the suite, and had thought he'd stop by, have a drink, and just relax a little until plane time.

Jo sensed his discomfort at having interrupted such an obvious rendezvous and—though uncomfortable herself about it—had tried to put him at ease. Then she had escaped into Alex's bedroom to dress. But now she suddenly sat down on the edge of his big, king-size bed and took a long, hard look around her.

The room was flamboyantly furnished, like everything else in the Floridiana. Lots of turquoise, black and silver. Art Deco bric-a-brac. Thick plush rugs and a heavy, quilted satin bedspread.

Her eyes roved around the room. How many times before had Alex set out to do exactly what he'd started to do with her this evening? How many swimming pools in posh resorts had he sat beside, with ladies far lovelier than she was? How many nightclubs had he frequented, with a stunning girl sharing his table? How many of those rendezvous had resulted in later ones in a room like this one?

He was so terribly attractive. And certainly anything but a monk. Had she really thought he'd been living his exciting life in celibacy?

Jo felt strangely chastened as she stuffed her bathing suit and terry robe into a tote bag she'd brought with her, gathered up her handbag and its contents, and then went back to the living room.

Alex had changed into slacks and a knit shirt. He'd made himself a drink, and he and Andy were sitting on a couch by the window engaged in deep conversation. Business talk, Jo felt sure.

Alex looked up, saw her, and immediately got to his feet. Andy followed suit, a bit more slowly. Jo felt herself being probed by both men's eyes as she put aside her handbag and the tote, and tried to appear very casual as she sat down on a bright purple chair.

"Drink?" Alex asked her.

She shook her head. "Thanks, no. I really must be getting on."

Andy Carson said hastily, "I'll be leaving in just a few minutes, Miss Bennett."

"Well, I imagine Alex will want to drive you to the airport, won't you, Alex?" she asked innocently.

She didn't dare meet Alex's eyes.

"I planned to take a cab," Andy said quickly.

"Maybe we could share it, then?" Jo offered. "It wouldn't be out of your way to drop me off. That way," she added pleasantly, "you won't need to have your car brought around, Alex."

He didn't answer her, and still hadn't spoken by the time the three of them moved toward the door. Then he merely said, "Thanks, Jo, for sharing your afternoon. Anytime you want to try out the pool again while I'm around, just let me know."

Jo, walking to the elevator at Andy's side, began to think she'd made a mistake. She couldn't expect Alex to understand why she was walking out like this, when, walking in, they'd both so clearly had the same thing in mind. Nor could she possibly tell him about the doubts that had plagued her while she was alone in his bedroom.

Downstairs, as she and Andy waited for a cab, Andy said cheerfully, "This is a real pleasure. And it gives me the chance to congratulate you personally on what your firm did for the Mimosa Mall. I think it's going to be Alex's best project to date.''

Jo nodded her agreement, and let Andy continue talking as they climbed into the cab, and during the short time it took to reach her condo.

Chapter Seven

Alex was furious. Livid. He couldn't remember when a woman had last made him so angry. And there wasn't a damned thing he could do about it.

He stared at the door he'd just closed behind Jo and Andy and resisted the impulse to take his fist to it and see if he could smash it to pieces. He strode over to the small portable bar that had come with the suite, found a clean glass, filled it with ice and splashed Scotch into it. He tried to make each movement deliberate, as if slowness and carefulness would assuage some of his anger.

They didn't.

He sat down on the purple chair and imagined he could smell Jo's perfume, even feel the warmth of her body. *Ridiculous!* he scoffed. *She probably doesn't have any warmth in her body. She's the coldest, most indifferent woman I've ever met!*

The still, small voice of conscience nagged, and he admitted to himself he was lying.

He glanced at his watch. It was quite early in the evening. There was time to arrange to go to dinner, a night club, a theater, almost anything. It was early enough to call Jo and say, "Hey, exactly what was that all about? Where were you coming from?"

He couldn't do it. There was such a thing as pride. And she'd really stung his.

He stared into space for a few empty minutes. Then he began pacing the living room like a caged tiger. Night settled over Sarasota. A tropical night, star-studded, complete with a mesmerizing moon. To make matters even worse, the reggae band was playing again out by the pool and the lilting music hit Alex, made him feel as if someone was twisting a rope inside him, around and around and around.

Jo had wanted him just as much as he'd wanted her. He *knew* it.

Nevertheless, he'd lost something with Jo at Fred Baxter's birthday party the other night. He'd give just about anything to recover that indefinable spirit that had existed between Jo and himself. One minute there was a wonderful sense of rapport between them, and the next there was a wall. He couldn't figure it out.

He'd approached the problem directly by asking her about it. She'd evaded an answer. So he'd cooled it all day Sunday and all day Monday, by exerting a maximum amount of self-control. He knew they'd be seeing each other at the mall opening Tuesday, and he'd hoped they could go on from there to straighten out whatever it was that had thrown a temporary block in their path.

But that was not the way it had worked out.

Despite the desire Jo had telegraphed to him, there'd still been an undercurrent of reserve about her today that had perplexed Alex. Except, perhaps, for that interval when they'd cavorted around in the pool. Could it be that Jo was running scared because, after all—as he'd pointed out himself—they'd known each other only a week?

God knows, *he* was running scared. It terrified him to think he was in critical danger of falling in love with Jo. In danger of loving, really loving a woman. That was something he'd never permitted himself before— the one time when he'd even come close had turned out to be no more than an adolescent fantasy. He'd been bruised, but had healed easily. Then he'd decided that real love, serious love, just wasn't in the cards for him.

He'd had a lot of interesting, adult relationships, he mused. And he supposed he'd had what most people would consider an unusually interesting life. Two lives, he amended.

He knew he'd have to tell Jo about Life One some day. Being a rock star when you were still basically a kid left its full share of scars. Though most of his scars had in fact been formed earlier. As Danny Forth he'd at least made a lot of money, and he'd had a great manager who had invested it wisely. Later, when it was necessary to change directions, he'd learned a few things about investing and business himself. That was when he'd found he had a flair for certain aspects of entrepreneurship, and Malls International, Ltd. had been born.

His manager, Ray Ellerson, was now retired and living in Arizona. But they still kept in touch, and sometimes Alex stopped over in Tucson on his trips to or from the West Coast.

Ray was the only person around who knew all there was to know about his two identities, Alex reflected. And felt a sudden need to talk to him.

It was still only late afternoon out in Arizona. He dialed. Ray answered on the second ring.

"Interrupt anything?" Alex asked.

"What were you expecting? That I was rendez-vousing with a leftover Folies Bergères star?" Ray shot back. "No, you're not interrupting anything except the repeat of an ice hockey game I didn't want to watch, anyway. Somehow ice hockey doesn't grab you when you live in Arizona the way it does when you live in New York. At least, that's my reaction." There was a pause. "Well, how's it going with you?"

"Great," Alex said. "That's to say, I guess it's great. We opened a new mall today."

"Where are you calling from?"

"Sarasota, Florida."

"Sarasota, eh? Used to be the home base of the Ringling Brothers and Barnum & Bailey Circus, didn't it?"

"Yes, I think so," Alex answered hoarsely.

"You don't sound too good." Ray seemed worried. "Anything wrong?"

"No, I'm fine," he said quickly. "Everything's fine. It's just that . . ."

"Yeah?"

"I think I'm in love," Alex confessed.

He was unprepared for the spate of swear words that crackled into his ear. "The hell you say. Who is she?"

"President and owner of a big operation here in Sarasota that specializes in plantscapes. Foliage designs. Outlays for malls and restaurants and—"

"I think I get the picture, son," Ray advised him dryly. "So you met her through business?"

Alex chuckled, remembering his first meeting with Jo. "Yes," he conceded.

"Isn't that against your usual policy? Seems to me I've heard you shout to the rafters that business and pleasure don't mix."

"This," Alex said slowly, "is different."

Ray digested that. Then said, "I can't believe this is coming from you. I'd like to meet her."

"Fly east tomorrow," Alex urged quickly. "I'm going to be in Sarasota through this week. I only plan to spend a couple of days in New York before I take off for China."

"China, this time?"

"Yes. But at the moment I don't especially want to go, even though it seemed pretty exciting until recently. Maybe I'll send Andy in my place."

"You *must* have it bad," Ray observed.

"I don't know what I have," Alex confessed. "You, more than anyone else, should know how this is hitting me."

"Son," Ray said, slowly, gently, "it was inevitable that at some time in your life you'd fall in love. I tried to tell you that."

"I guess it was the one thing you've ever told me I didn't believe."

"No, there's something else I guess you didn't believe," Ray contradicted him. "I tried to tell you it's crazy to think every woman in the world is like your mother, or even that show girl who dumped you. You can't blame an entire sex for one woman's folly!"

"Can't you?" Alex asked quietly.

"I know *you* have," Ray answered him. "Otherwise you probably would have fallen for more of the girls who were chasing you. But you never could bring yourself to trust them."

"Would you have, if you'd been in my place?"

"I don't know," Ray mumbled. "I honest to God don't know. If I'd had your mother and Aunt Laura as examples..."

"When I look back, I can't blame Aunt Laura," Alex said soberly. "I was nine when I was dumped on her, and she'd never had any kids around before. I wasn't even her blood relative, just her husband's nephew. She didn't know how to handle me, and I didn't know how to approach her."

Ray snorted disbelief. "Alex, after the stories you've told me over the years, I honestly doubt that woman even attempted to approach you. Hell, she wouldn't even talk to you *after* you made it big! And," he continued, "what about when your uncle died? Remember? I was there when you finally got that phone call—*after* the funeral."

Alex reached for the glass he'd set aside, and took a long swallow of Scotch. "Hell," he said, "let's get onto another subject. I guess you know that one by heart, anyway." He heaved a sigh. "Anyway, I'll never really know what Laura really thought, will I? It's too late for speculation now.''

He was surprised at how much it still hurt to dredge up the old memories of his Uncle Ralph and Aunt Laura, to say nothing of his parents. He'd been seven when his mother left town with another man. His father, a successful lawyer in Burlington, Vermont, had virtually gone out of his mind over his wife's desertion. He'd hired a team of private detectives to find her. When they did, almost two years later, Alex's mother had already divorced Harold Grant and was married to the man she'd run off with—Harold's best friend, someone he'd known since boyhood.

In his grief and desperation, Harold had gone out to the garage at the back of his house in the dead of winter, sealed up all the doors and windows, then had turned on his car motor and gone to sleep forever.

Ralph Grant, Harold's brother, also lived in Burlington. He was an accountant, well respected in the community, but an unusually private person. Though Ralph took some part in civic activities, Alex couldn't remember him and his wife Laura ever having any kind of social life. They were grim, straitlaced people, set in their ways. As he'd just said to Ray, there'd been no place in their lives for a nine-year-old orphan.

Ralph had been more accepting than Laura about having a young boy in the house. He'd even tried now and then to have some rapport with Alex. Alex could remember a couple of occasions when his uncle had taken him fishing. Laura, on the other hand, had become even more resentful of and frustrated with him as time went by. It had all culminated in a never-to-be-forgotten guitar-smashing incident that had been just one of many events designed to hurt him. Mentally and emotionally, if not physically.

It didn't stop him, though. He delivered more newspapers in the cold Vermont winter, saved up more money, bought another old acoustic guitar. But he'd sneaked off to quiet, hidden places in which to play it. He'd learned his lesson.

He sighed, and Ray said, "Son? Look, tell me about this girl."

"Jo?"

"For Josephine?"

"Yes."

"My mother's name was Josephine," Ray said solemnly. "If she's anything like my mother, you've got yourself a real jewel, Alex."

Alex smiled sadly. Ray had talked to him before about his mother, who'd died a couple of years before he and Alex had met. Part of the talk, he'd suspected, had been to try to show him that not all women would let down their husbands and children the way *his* mother had let down his father and himself.

Hell, he had the sense to know that not everyone's mother was an immoral witch, nor was everyone's aunt sadistic and frustrated. It was just that when it came to the thought of becoming seriously involved with a woman he still ran scared. A woman would have to prove herself to him, insofar as loyalty and love were concerned. But he didn't doubt it was possible for that to happen. He just had to be very, very sure, that was all.

Ray said, again, "Alex? Hey, are you still there?"

"Yes," Alex said quickly. "Sorry."

"Are you going to tell me about this Josephine?"

"She's very lovely," Alex said huskily. "A figure that would send your blood pressure sky-high. Gorgeous dark eyes. Amber-colored hair."

"Amber-colored, yet?"

"Yes, it really is. I keep kidding her that she's small, but actually she's medium height. Smart. Very smart. When her father died a couple of years ago, she took over as president of his company, and she runs the firm herself.

"And," Alex continued, "she's gutsy. She doesn't mind standing up to a person if she thinks she's right. Sticks up for her employees. She's a fighter, Ray. I was an important client to her, but she didn't hesitate to tell me off the first time we met."

"Is she still telling you off, Alex?"

"I guess maybe, in a way," Alex said uncomfortably. "We went out the other night to a party for a friend of hers. Something I said or did turned her off. Problem is, I can't get her to tell me what it is...."

His voice was growing hoarser. Quietly, Ray said, "I'd kind of appreciate it if you'd check out with a throat specialist."

Alex had a sudden, vivid recollection of the first time Ray had ever said that to him. It had been in Chicago, where he was playing a major solo concert. He'd awakened that morning to find it was all he could do to swallow. His throat felt odd. It didn't hurt. It was just...uncomfortable.

He'd gone on as usual that night and brought down the house. The fans either hadn't noticed the added huskiness in his voice, or else they'd liked it. Afterward, in his hotel suite, Alex had immediately gone into the bathroom and gargled with a lot of hot water mixed with an antiseptic. His voice had been so hoarse after the exertion of the concert that he could barely speak.

Ray had been waiting for him when he came out of the bathroom. "I think we'd better get ourselves to a throat specialist," Ray had said solemnly.

And that appointment with the throat specialist had spelled the end of everything for Danny Forth. But out of those ashes, Alex reminded himself, he'd been reborn. And he knew in all honesty he wouldn't go back, even if he could.

Jo stretched out on the bed in her condo, turned over onto her right side then flipped to her left side. After tossing and turning for what seemed like hours, she got up, went to the kitchen and took a can of beer out of the refrigerator.

She wasn't much of a beer drinker—she wasn't much of a drinker at all, for that matter—but she recalled someone had told her a while back that beer at bedtime helped you go to sleep.

Jo took her beer into the living room, curled up in an armchair by the window, and sipped slowly. The big living-room picture window looked out over Sarasota Bay. Far to the left she could see the lights on the Ringling Causeway that led from the city to Lido and St. Armand's and Longboat Keys, part of the chain of narrow, barrier islands off this section of the Florida Gulf Coast.

She could see lights twinkling in homes and condos over on the keys, and she felt a surge of loneliness. She reminded herself sharply that she wasn't alone. She had friends around Sarasota, lots of friends. She could put together a party at a moment's notice.

Yet, she conceded, it was a while since she'd been really close to anyone. Not because she was antisocial but because, since her father's death, she'd had both hands so full. It had taken all her time and energy to get the business firmly organized—things had slipped a bit, in that respect, during her father's long illness—and it was only recently that she'd felt able to let up a little.

Now the time was coming when maybe she could afford to play a little. Relax. Maybe even let someone into her life.

Someone? The only person she'd wanted to even open the door a crack for, since she could remember, was Alex Grant.

And what about Alex?

Ever since Andy Carson had dropped her off at the downstairs door to the condo, she'd been reproaching herself for walking out on Alex as she had tonight. Damn it, she'd reneged... in the worst way. She couldn't blame him if he crossed her off his list.

She'd been unfair to Alex, very unfair. She hadn't even given him a chance to explain his fib of the other night. A small fib that seemed less and less consequential when she thought of it rationally. Alex had the right not to sing if he didn't want to. And to pass that off in a way that would cause the least comment.

Now part of her problem was that she'd been embarrassed when they'd walked into Alex's suite and found Andy waiting there. She felt certain it wouldn't have taken a clairvoyant to have sensed there'd been something very specific on both her mind and Alex's. Maybe there was an unsuspected vein of prudery in her nature and that was what had bothered her so much. Though Andy certainly had neither done nor said anything to fuel her embarrassment. Very much the contrary, in fact.

Nevertheless, just because she was chagrined it didn't give her the excuse to leap to conclusions, as she had done in his bedroom.

She was judging Alex by a single statement that might be considered a fib, and by the *possibilities* inherent in his life-style.

She went back to her bedroom and picked up the luminous clock from the bedside table. It was a quarter past two. Though she yearned to call Alex and explain her erratic behavior, it was too late to do so.

Reluctantly, Jo went back to bed and tried everything from counting sheep to blacking out her mind in an effort to get to sleep again. Nothing worked. An image of Alex kept intruding. It was a long while before she finally dozed off.

In his suite at the Floridiana, Alex was having an equally hard time getting any sleep.

The phone conversation with Ray, though therapeutic in some ways, had revived a lot of old, painful memories.

After a time, Alex went into the kitchenette and heated a cup of milk in the microwave. Then he wandered into the living room and stared out into the black and silver night, suddenly aware of how fundamentally empty his life was, for all of his work, wealth, friends, exciting opportunities....

For most of the years he could remember, he'd never been really close to anyone, except Ray. Probably his father hadn't intended to make him hate his mother, but he'd done so, even if subconsciously. And he'd never been really close to his father. Especially after his wife's desertion, Harold Grant had become withdrawn. A tormented person who had no room for a young son in his shattered life.

Then the unhappy years had followed—nearly seven of them—with his Uncle Ralph and Aunt Laura.

Shifting restlessly as he sipped the warm milk, Alex remembered sneaking out of his uncle's house when he was sixteen years old. He'd clutched a guitar, a tote bag stuffed with his clothes and a few other odds and ends, and in his pocket he had a wallet with his total worldly wealth in it. Fifty-four dollars and eighty-six cents.

At the edge of town, he'd begun to hitchhike. Maybe it was the guitar, maybe just his clean, youthful looks, but he was lucky enough to get rides that took him as far as Albany, New York. And it was there that his career as Danny Forth had begun.

He started to play, whenever and wherever he could. He wandered from Albany through a series of small towns, playing in parks, playing on street corners, playing any place he could find—with his guitar case open at his feet for people to toss coins into—until, more often than not, the cops chased him away.

He began to do gigs with local groups whenever they'd let him in—as they did more and more often, because he was very good. It wasn't so much his guitar playing. He considered himself just a cut or so above mediocre on the guitar, though he got better as

128

time went by. It was his singing. He had a terrific voice—young, gutsy, different, as were his methods of onstage song delivery. He'd been through a lot by the age of sixteen. He let it all show in his voice, let the raw, suppressed emotions take over his music, pouring his heart into his songs, many of which he wrote himself.

He learned about a lot of things fast. There was no slow lane in the life he'd chosen. He learned how to fake an identity that would make him out to be three years older than he was. And which showed his name as Danny Forth.

Finally he started getting better and better gigs. Then one steady band began backing him. An agent discovered him. He met Ray. A deal was made for him to cut an album with a major recording company. And his career took off.

By the time he was twenty-three, he was sitting on top of the world, and there were no competitors close enough to be able to shove him off that pinnacle.

Then one morning he woke up and found it was hard to swallow. . . .

Alex drained his cup of milk, put his hand to his throat and massaged it lightly. A reflex gesture, because even now he never took swallowing entirely for granted.

By that terrible morning, he'd had it all—fame, fortune, everything but love, he bitterly reminded himself now. There had always been girls. Hundreds of girls. Young women had screamed themselves hoarse over him wherever he went, literally trying to stampede him, desperate to get a lock of his hair or a bead off his necklace.

It had come to the point where he was surrounded by bodyguards whenever he left the stage after a performance. With such adulation, it was easy to become conceited. Easy to take all kinds of favors very lightly.

Even then, Alex had never confused infatuation or excitement or lust with love, except for that single time when he'd let himself indulge in fantasy. And it was an aberration he had quickly recovered from.

But after that terrible morning when he first knew there was something seriously wrong with his throat, he'd quickly discovered, the hard way, how fast stars could fall. He could have written a book about the fickleness of fans, and how quickly one can be abandoned, left alone, once the entertainment world's cold spotlight shifts.

Only Ray had stuck with him. Then, and all the way up again as he rose to the top in an entirely different arena.

He wondered now what might have happened if, way back then, he'd known Jo.

Chapter Eight

Jo couldn't wait any longer. She'd been up since six o'clock pacing her apartment, trying to wish away time until it would be late enough to call Alex. Now she decided eight o'clock was late enough.

His phone rang three times. She was about to hang up—assuming maybe he'd gone for an early-morning swim or, after last night, had decided to choose a place other than Sarasota for the remainder of his vacation—when he answered.

She said contritely, "I woke you up."

"Jo!"

Jo pictured him propped up against a pillow as he spoke. Probably needing a shave. His dark hair tousled. His eyes still sleepy. It was an emotion-boggling vision, all she needed for those treacherous little ribbons of desire to start weaving through her.

"Alex." Jo paused. "Alex," she began again, "I'm sorry. I know it's still early, but I didn't want to miss you."

Alex chuckled. "Was I going somewhere?"

"I—I don't know," she stammered.

"Jo, sweetheart, what could be better than waking up to the sound of your voice?" Alex asked huskily. "I wouldn't care what time it was."

Jo wished she'd called him around three o'clock that morning after all.

"As for my going anywhere, no, I'm not going anywhere," he told her. "I'm not even sure what day it is. That's what happens to a man when he's on vacation. His mind gets weak."

"That'd be something, the day your mind ever gets weak," Jo muttered. "Alex, look, I have to go to work today. Some potential clients are flying over from the East Coast. I really need to talk to them myself."

"Jo," Alex said gently, "I didn't expect you to take a holiday because I decided to take one."

"Well," Jo said, "I—I wish I could. I wish I could be with you."

"Right now?"

"Yes," she admitted.

"Sometimes," Alex said, "I guess I don't entirely understand you."

He sounded baffled. She couldn't blame him. Not very many hours ago she'd walked out of his hotel suite under circumstances a lot of men would find difficult to forgive.

Suddenly she made up her mind she was going to tell him about that small remark he'd made at Fred's that had upset her out of all proportion. And . . . she was going to tell him she knew who he was.

No, she decided. She wasn't going to tell him. She was going to *show* him.

"Look," she said, "it's hard to explain things over the phone. At least, it is for me. I usually do a better job of it face-to-face."

"I consider one of life's optimum conditions finding myself face-to-face with you," Alex murmured.

She didn't pick him up on that. Right now, she didn't want to flirt with him. "Alex," she began again.

"Yes, Jo?" There was a note of hidden laughter in his husky voice.

"What's so funny?" she asked suspiciously.

"The way you just said 'Alex'. . .it sounded as if you were about to make some sort of pronouncement," he teased. Then sobered. "Guess maybe that isn't so funny, after all."

Jo took the plunge. "I just wanted to ask you to come over to my place for dinner tonight," she said.

There was silence. The seconds ticked by. Jo told herself she should have known that Alex wouldn't be eager to accept an invitation from her after last night, despite the easy way he'd been handling her phone call.

She said, "Look, Alex, it's okay. I mean, if you have other plans . . ."

He said patiently, "Jo, love, didn't I just tell you I have nothing at all on my schedule for the rest of my time in Sarasota? Do I need to spell that out for you? What it means is that all I want . . ."

"Yes?"

"All I want is to be with you as much as *you* can be with me," he said honestly. "But you're going to have to set the pace this time around, Jo. I don't know what happened yesterday, I don't know what happened Saturday night. I can only hope you'll fill me in...."

"I will," she promised, her voice very small.

"Regardless, I don't want you to do anything you don't want to do," Alex said very seriously.

She laughed wryly. "I'm a big girl, Alex."

"In some ways, yes," he agreed. "I have the feeling in other ways you're still a babe in the woods. The last thing I'd want to do is hurt you, Jo. If I came on too strong... I'm sorry."

"I think we were both coming on in pretty much the same way," Jo told him frankly.

"Thanks for saying that," he said, his voice huskier than ever. "Most women wouldn't."

"Older women, maybe," she conceded.

"Most women," he corrected. "Anyway..."

"Alex," Jo said carefully, "I know you don't want to hurt me." She did know it. What worried her was what he was leading to by spelling it out this way. Was he warning her that he had just this single week out of his life to share with her? Was he cueing her in on the fact that he wasn't one for commitments? He was what? Thirty-five? She didn't doubt he had his life very much under control. Probably tailored exactly the way he wanted it.

"Alex, look," she said. "I'm not saying we should start over again tonight. I wouldn't give up what's already happened between us. We're two adults, we're attracted to each other, we enjoy each other's company. Right?"

"Mmm," Alex mused. "I would certainly say so."

Was he teasing her again? Jo couldn't be sure.

Suddenly sounding very businesslike, he asked, "What time do you want me to come around tonight, Jo?"

She was startled by the acquiescence she'd stopped expecting. "How about seven?" she managed.

"Fine. Can I bring anything?"

"Just yourself," Jo answered. The thought of Alex filling her small condo with his charismatic presence brought an unexpected nervousness, and she could only manage a rather feeble, "See you then," before she hung up.

The morning passed quickly at Greenscapes. Jo handled four long-distance phone calls from people interested in talking with her about her firm's services, then had a fifth call from her cousin Tim, who wanted to talk to her about a couple of small problems that had come up in the new Miami office. She'd been through the same experiences Tim was having, and was quickly able to reassure him.

"I think I have the world's smartest and prettiest cousin," Tim stated before they rang off.

"Flatterer," she said with a laugh. She and Tim were both only children. He was the son of her father's older brother who, several years ago, had crashed in his small plane when he flew into a patch of unexpected bad weather in central Florida. Tim was a couple of years younger than Jo. He'd been about thirteen when his father died. After that, he'd often come visiting at Greenscapes. Clark Bennett had been something of a surrogate father to him. So Dad's death had been almost as traumatic for Tim as it had for her, Jo reflected.

Tim's mother had remarried and moved to St. Petersburg, but Jo knew Tim didn't see very much of her. He wasn't especially fond of his stepfather. After the opening of the Miami office, Jo had asked him if he'd like to head it, and he had welcomed the chance.

Her phone conversations finished for the time being, Jo turned her attention to some urgent paperwork. After a while she closed her eyes wearily, wishing there might be a chance to snatch an afternoon nap, something that would ordinarily never occur to her. But she wanted to be refreshed and bright-eyed when Alex came to dinner tonight. She had a full day ahead, though; there was not likely to be time for any snoozing.

At eleven o'clock Jo met with a client who wanted to open a new dinner theater complex in the area. He was aware he had competition, but he also had some innovative ideas of his own and his enthusiasm was catching.

Jo liked this aspect of business, this bouncing back of ideas. One idea so often triggered another, and it became a real game.

Time slipped by. The potential client was in his early fifties, he'd already talked about his wife with affection—something always nice to hear—and had told her he had twin daughters, now in their second year of college. When he checked his watch, observed that it was well past noon, and asked if she could possibly have lunch with him, she found herself saying yes.

They drove to a waterfront restaurant not far from the Floridiana. In fact, they passed the Floridiana on their way, and as Jo's eyes swept the big rococo hotel complex she wondered if Alex was lounging by the swimming pool, or indulging in a strawberry daiquiri at the thatched-roof bar.

Fiercely she wished that she were with him.

It was nearly two-thirty when the theater owner delivered Jo back to the Greenscapes office. She'd not intended to take so much time away from her desk, but she had the satisfaction of knowing that the luncheon had cemented things to the point where she now had a new client. Greenscapes was to be retained to do the floral designs for the theater complex. It was going to be a challenging job, a lot of fun—and also was going to require a lot of clever planning. She decided she'd talk over the plan that was forming in her mind with Fred. This, she thought happily, was something he could free-lance for her. Maybe work on in collaboration with one of the other designers on Greenscapes' staff.

Jo arrived at her office to find that a few problems had preceded her. Marge had a raft of phone messages for her, all marked Urgent. Then Bob Hawley had left word that he needed to see her as soon as she came in.

Jo suspected that Bob was still chagrined about the original fiasco at Mimosa Mall. He'd been working under Len, and he'd told her frankly that he felt it should be considered his goof. Jo had assured him it wasn't any single individual's fault. She'd said they'd all take whatever blame had to be taken and—as it happened—the project had, of course, had an extremely happy ending.

She discovered now that Bob was running just a bit scared since the Mimosa fiasco. He wanted her to come out and personally inspect a shipment of exotic foliage recently arrived at Greenscapes.

"I don't think it's up to snuff," he muttered worriedly.

"Bob," Jo replied, trying to be patient because she could appreciate that he was still a bit edgy, "you *know* if it's up to snuff or not. If the quality isn't right, return it."

"This is a nursery that supplies us regularly," Bob told her. "Everything we've ever gotten from them has been top quality. Jo, I'd really appreciate it if you'd take a look yourself."

Bob was another person who'd been around Greenscapes for a long time. Not as long as Len, but long enough. Her father had considered him one of his best men. So she went along with him.

She switched the beige pumps she'd worn to lunch for a pair of old sneakers she kept in her office for just such occasions as this, and spent the better part of the next hour going over the new stock with Bob. Her diagnosis was that perhaps the plants had suffered some slight shock in shipment, but that they were basically fine. "All they need is a little TLC and regular anointing with Greenscapes water," she assured Bob with a smile.

Bob smiled back. "You must think I'm going over the edge, Jo," he admitted.

"Not at all," she assured him quickly.

"I felt so rotten about the Mimosa job," he said. "Especially in view of Len's illness—"

"Look," Jo stated firmly. "If everything came out as well in the end as the Mimosa job did we'd never have to worry about anything. Forget it, Bob. It doesn't do to look back, when there's so much ahead."

"That sounds like something your father would have said," Bob observed.

"Well, I hope some of Dad's wisdom rubbed off on me," Jo acknowledged. "I could use a lot more of it."

Bob reached over and patted her shoulder. "You're doing just fine," he told her, and she felt herself actually swelling with pride. Words like that from people like Bob were the highest form of praise.

Back in her office again, she tried to tackle the urgent messages one by one, including dictating a couple of priority letters Marge could type first thing in the morning.

She couldn't believe it when Marge loomed up in the office doorway to ask, "Are you going to stay here all night?"

"No," Jo said hastily. She glanced at her wristwatch and moaned. It was almost six o'clock.

"Why are you still hanging around here?" she asked her secretary.

"Waiting for the boss to leave."

"Marge," Jo protested, "you should know better than that. Anyway, this is one time I wish you'd told me to cut out."

"A special evening ahead?" Marge asked with a twinkle in her eye.

"Yes, as a matter of fact. I invited Alex to come for dinner and I'm supposed to cook.

"What time is he coming?" Marge asked.

"Seven."

"Jo, that's fifty-five minutes from now," her secretary pointed out. "You'd better get on the road."

Jo made a hasty exit, leaving Marge to close up. She called at the liquor store in a small corner shopping complex, stopped by a bakery she favored, and was three-quarters of the way home when something happened to her that had never happened before.

She got a flat tire.

She was driving in heavy traffic when she heard a loud hiss. When the car started to thump and lurch she realized sickly what the problem must be and managed to edge over to the curb.

An elderly man in the car behind her followed, and was so sympathetic that Jo wanted to break down and wail on his shoulder. He promised to send someone back from the nearest gas station to help her out. Jo, not much for anything mechanical, had not even the vaguest idea of how to change a tire herself.

The auto mechanic from the gas station arrived within ten minutes, but it seemed like ten hours to Jo. He put on her spare for her, then wanted her to go back to the station with him so he could check out the damaged tire to see if it could be salvaged.

She couldn't have cared less. "Just toss it in the trunk," she said hurriedly, "and I'll have it looked at tomorrow."

"From the way you describe it, you probably ran over glass, or maybe some sharp metal," the mechanic opined. "Lot of construction work going around here, too. Could be a nail...."

"Whatever," Jo said. Then, realizing the man had put himself out for her, coming to her rescue in the middle of a top-of-the-season rush hour, she forced a smile, paid him, and gave him a liberal tip. After that, it was all she could do to keep from breaking the speed limit as she covered the distance to her condo. The way her luck was going, she muttered to herself a police car would undoubtedly be heading in the other direction, spot her, swing around and give her a ticket.

She pulled into the parking lot at the condo at twenty-five minutes past seven.

As she emerged from her car, clutching the bottle of wine and the loaf of bread, a tall figure disengaged itself from the shadows and sauntered toward her.

"Thought that was you," Alex said pleasantly.

"Alex, I'm so sorry," Jo moaned. "Everything happened today. I mean, just everything. Then, would you believe it, on the way over here I got a flat tire, and—"

"Hey," Alex admonished. "You're running out of breath. Easy, Jo. It's no big deal."

"But I've kept you waiting...."

"You're worth waiting for," he told her softly.

He reached over, took the packages out of her arms, and waited for her to precede him. She caught the whiff of a scent she was beginning to identify with him. After-shave, probably. A very faint, sort of woodsy aroma. She would have sworn she could feel the warmth of him, just a step or so behind her...and having him so near was overwhelming.

Whatever happened after tonight...she wanted him, Jo admitted to herself. Admitted it fully. She was ready to face up to the uncertainty of tomorrow if she could be with him tonight.

I'm not going to muff this again, she promised herself.

Once they were in the condo, her apologies tumbled out. "Somehow this day just got away from me," she told Alex. "I was late leaving the office, then I had the flat tire on the way home. I've never had one before!"

"You sound like it's an invasion of privacy," Alex said smiling. "Jo, love, flat tires or things akin to them happen to all of us, from time to time."

"But to have it happen *tonight*," she moaned.

"The night's still young," Alex said easily.

Another thought suddenly hit Jo. She faced him, dismayed. "You must be starving," she told him.

"Reasonably hungry, but not starving," he answered, giving her the full impact of his lopsided grin.

"Alex, it's going to take a while for me to put our dinner together. I mean, I was just going to whip up some spaghetti but I have to make the sauce and—"

"Why not give me a rain check on the spaghetti and we'll go out somewhere?" he suggested.

Jo didn't want to go out. There was nothing more that she wanted than to stay home with Alex. The two of them cozy and comfortable and alone.

"Wouldn't you rather stay home?" she asked.

At the word "home," an odd expression crept into Alex's blue-gray eyes. Wistfulness? Regret? Jo couldn't quite define it. She knew only that the word had had a decided effect on Alex and when he answered her his voice was a bit unsteady. "When you put it that way," he said, "yes."

"Look," she suggested, "why don't you fix your-self a Scotch and soda and relax while I get things going in the kitchen?"

He smiled. "I have a better idea."

"And what might that be?"

"Let's combine the best of two alternatives," Alex told her. "I noticed there's a Chinese restaurant a couple of streets over. Why don't I call up and have them prepare a take-out order for us? Then while you're fixing the drinks I'll go pick it up?"

Jo laughed. "That's an offer I can't refuse."

By the time Alex came back with several cartons of Chinese food, Jo had slipped into a pale green caf-tan, brushed her hair into shining waves around her shoulders, and daubed just a hint of her best perfume behind her earlobes.

She saw Alex's eyebrows rise slightly at his first glimpse of her, nor could she blame him for being a little bit surprised. She was presenting a different Jo Bennett—but this was the Jo Bennett she wanted to present to him tonight. While he'd glimpsed some-thing of her personal side, he'd seen enough of her business side. Tonight she wanted him to get to know all of her. As she wanted to get to know all of him.

It was an oversimplification to say that she wanted to clear the air between them. What she wanted to do was lead him into telling her about his Danny Forth identity. Before this night was over she wanted to sweep all curtains aside.

It was her plan, when the moment seemed right, to slip on one of the tapes she'd made from her Danny Forth albums. Surely Alex would have to come out and say something then.

The right moment just didn't seem to be when they were eating the Chinese food Alex had brought. For one thing, he'd purchased chopsticks and insisted they both use them. Jo's awkward attempts provided them both with amusement, and, with laughter and patience, Alex taught her how to deftly wield the chopsticks.

He had also bought some plum wine to go with the food. Between the wine and having Alex put his hand over hers every time he corrected her finger position with the chopsticks, she was more than a little giddy by the time the meal was over.

She remembered that she had some Japanese melon liqueur and brought it out to serve with the almond cookies Alex had bought for their dessert.

So far she'd been playing a variety of music on the stereo. Now she turned the lights down low and came close to deciding to postpone playing a Danny Forth tape for another time. She didn't want to do anything that would destroy the light mood between them. But on the other hand she knew there had to be no doubts in her mind about Alex if she were going to give herself to him tonight.

Jo literally gritted her teeth, changed the tape...and then sank back and waited.

Her condo was suddenly filled with a new kind of sound. A voice she'd never forget filled the room with the songs of her youth. She knew if she closed her eyes she'd see Danny Forth putting his heart, his soul, everything he had into his singing....

Alex was sitting in a chair near the window. Behind him, the moon arced over Sarasota Bay. There was a lamp turned low on a table near him, but his face was partially in shadow. Jo could not read his expression. But she saw Alex flinch as if he'd been stung. The tiny glass of pale green liqueur wobbled in his hand, and she thought he was about to drop it.

Then Alex steadied, and he seemed to merely be listening to the music. Jo, sitting on the edge of the couch, her emotions frazzled, waited for him to speak. But when he did, what he said had nothing to do with Danny Forth.

Chapter Nine

Jo couldn't believe what she was hearing. Alex was saying something about having met with a real estate agent that afternoon who'd shown him several Siesta Key properties available for sale.

After a moment in which she'd actually *felt* the shock emanating from him as he heard the tape, he'd picked up a conversational thread as if nothing had happened.

"I gather there are quite a few places for sale on the key," he said casually, while music continued to throb in the background. "I plan to take a look at some others tomorrow. Actually, the second place I saw this afternoon was rather nice. It was on a canal, with its own boat dock. It might be fun to have a boat so you could go out and do some fishing in the gulf."

Jo felt the pretty pink world she'd been building up around herself dissolve. So much for romance, so much for illusion, she thought bitterly. So much for honesty.

She could sit still no longer. She switched a nearby three way lamp to full power and turned off the stereo.

Glancing toward Alex, she saw him staring at her in surprise.

"What was all that about?" he asked mildly.

How could he be such a ... *dissembler*. She fought back anger and disappointment as she challenged him. "Don't you know?"

"Know what, Jo?" he asked. "I don't think I'm following you."

She waved toward the stereo. "Back in those days, Alex," she said, as if his music were still playing, "I was one of your biggest fans."

The silence between them became lead-heavy.

Alex stood and turned the lamp nearest him up to full power, too. Viewing him in the glare of that much brighter light, Jo saw that he looked like someone suddenly... stricken. Tired. Older.

Suddenly she wished she could back out of this whole situation, rewind the evening to the moment before she'd put on the Danny Forth tapes... and then put on some other tapes instead. But when Alex turned his gaze on her, she knew it was too late.

It was too late. Alex couldn't possibly have defined his own feelings. He, too, would have given a lot to rewind this particular evening... but for different reasons. If he had it to do over again, he would have gotten down to his autobiography well before now.

Why had it never occurred to him that she might have been one of his fans? She was the right age. He'd been big with the teeny boppers who, in those days, had so gone out of their minds over rock stars.

Damn! he thought savagely. Why did this have to happen here? Now?

The irony of it was that the legend of Danny Forth wasn't even a secret he'd wanted to keep from her. Danny Forth was—had been, he corrected—a part of him. A big part. If he and Jo were going any distance together, she needed to know about that part. She needed to know about *all* of him. As he needed to know about all of her.

But the meteoric rise and fall of Danny Forth wasn't a subject he'd been ready to get into tonight. Tonight he had wanted to be with her, just the two of them, with no encroachments. He had wanted to make love to her. And everything about Jo—the tenor of her invitation, the way she'd been dressed when he came back with the Chinese food—had indicated she shared exactly the same needs and desires.

"When did you find out?" he asked hoarsely.

Jo sank back in her chair again. She was on the edge of both anger and tears. Her emotions were so tangled that they were shooting off in a dozen different directions.

She said unsteadily, "It wasn't a question of finding out. I recognized you that first day at the mall."

Alex stared at her, shocked. "I'll be damned," he muttered disbelievingly. And then added bitterly, "Why you? Why you, of all people?"

"What do you mean?"

"Would you believe no one else has ever recognized me, Jo?"

"They would, if you moved in different circles. You've been moving in corporate circles, with older people, I imagine."

"I guess so. Regardless."

"As I said, I was one of your biggest fans," Jo admitted unhappily. "I never had the chance to see you in concert, but I followed your career every step of the way. Watched you every time you were on TV, listened to you every time you were on radio, bought all your albums, read every word written about you. Me," she finished, "and I guess thousands of other people my age."

Alex closed his eyes wearily, then opened them again and looked at her reproachfully. "Why didn't you say something until now?" he asked her. "Why didn't you say something *now*, for that matter? What did you think was going to happen when you played that tape? Did you expect me to leap to my feet, shouting, 'That's me, that's me!'"

"I guess I thought hearing the music might provoke a reaction in you."

"Well, if that's what you wanted, you succeeded, didn't you?" he taunted. "Hell, if you wondered so much, why didn't you come out and ask me?"

"I couldn't," Jo said simply.

He shook his head. "Female logic escapes me," he admitted wryly. "Always has, and I guess it always will. The planning you did astonishes me. Setting up this whole scene, getting yourself into something soft and sexy, coming on to me like all you wanted was for the two of us to make this a night we'd remember forever. Well, I'll remember it forever, but not in the way I expected to.''

"Alex—"

"Jo, don't sound so hurt. How did you think I'd react?''

"I wasn't trying to set you up," she protested.

"Then I'd hate to see what might happen if you did try. You went to an awful lot of trouble just to get a simple answer.''

Jo's lips trembled and tears spilled over. Surveying her, Alex said dryly, "Spare me. You can turn off the tears, Jo. I think it was rotten of you to handle this as you did. And you can go ahead and cry all night, if you like. It won't change my opinion.''

Jo turned abruptly and went out to her tiny kitchen. A moment later he heard the sound of running water.

He followed her to the kitchen door. Jo, her back to him, was filling her coffee maker with water and coffee. She'd already set out cups, saucers and spoons. As he watched, she plugged in the coffee maker.

"What's the matter?" Alex asked. "Do you suddenly need a caffeine fix?''

She swung around, surveying him tautly. Even her muscles felt tense. It was a question either of maintaining rigidity or of going to pieces altogether. After his caustic comments, she was damned if she was going to let him see her cry again.

She snapped, "I thought we could both use some coffee.''

"Speak for yourself," Alex said. "I've been staying awake nights enough as it is. If anything, I'd go for some Scotch on the rocks.''

Jo yanked the cord out of the outlet with an impatient tug. She opened the freezer door and took out the ice cubes. "Would you mind fixing your own drink?" she asked him.

"No," he replied. "And I didn't mean to keep you from having some coffee, Jo, if you want it."

"I think I'll have a drink myself," she decided.

Watching her fix herself a vodka and tonic, Alex felt himself beginning to melt. She looked so small, so tense...and so hurt.

It had not occurred to him that keeping his Danny Forth identity from her might have hurt her.

"Jo..." he began, mentally stumbling around as he tried to find the right words.

"It's okay, Alex," Jo said tightly. "There's no reason for you to say anything...about it."

"I want to say a lot about it," Alex announced, and discovered that he did want exactly that. It was crazy to let someone who'd been a ghost for over a decade come between them.

"I don't think it would be wise," Jo declared. "We're both...somewhat on edge. If there's any talking to be done it would be better done at another time."

"I don't agree," Alex said levelly. "Look, let's go sit down and get this over with."

He looked very grave and very tired. Jo felt a sudden stab of self-reproach. What was she doing to him?

"No, Alex," she said suddenly. "We don't have to talk about it...ever."

"Oh, God," Alex moaned. "Look, I know all the old saws about women and their mind changing but this is a little much, Jo. You've led into this. Hell, you *plunged* into it. What do you think I'm going to do now? Put it on a back burner again?"

She shook her head. "No, I'm willing to forget all about the past," she said with difficulty. "Let's start over, right now, Alex."

"And go to bed with each other?" he asked bluntly.

Jo flushed. "Let's just . . . start over," she urged.

"And forget that I was Danny Forth and you had a teenage crush on me?"

"Yes," she said desperately.

"I think you know how impossible that is," he said with an outward calm that was belied by the tense muscle Jo saw twisting near his jaw. "Come on, Jo. You want to know. I'm prepared to tell you. But I think there's something we should come to an agreement about before we start."

"What?" she asked faintly.

"Danny Forth's dead, Jo."

Alex, Scotch in hand, was walking toward the living room as he said that. Jo stared at his retreating back. She'd certainly rushed in where angels feared to tread, she told herself bitterly. Reluctantly she followed him.

Alex stretched out in an armchair, surveyed the tips of his brown loafers, coddled his glass of Scotch. He said, "You did hear what I just said to you, didn't you, Jo? Danny Forth's dead."

Jo sank into the corner of her couch. "That's not so and you know it," she managed to say after a moment.

"Ah, but it is so. There is nothing of Danny Forth about me. Can you understand that? I'm an entirely different person."

"I don't understand why you'd want to say Danny's dead." Her voice shook slightly. "Unless... unless he did something so terrible toward the end of his career that you've had to blot it out...."

Alex looked startled. Then he said with a wry smile, "You'll be bringing out the inkblot tests next. Danny Forth did nothing terrible. He got an especially rotten break, that's all."

A wave of relief washed over Jo. She'd built up so many stories that would be hurtful to this man sitting across from her. To this man she loved...

The telltale words echoed. Jo flinched slightly as she registered them, because they made her feel so vulnerable. But... she did love Alex. And her love for Alex had nothing at all to do with Danny Forth.

She wished she could find a way to tell him that.

He asked suddenly, "Haven't you ever wondered about my voice?"

"Your voice?" she was honestly surprised.

"Haven't you noticed that most of the time I sound as if I'm right on the edge of laryngitis?" he persisted.

"Your voice is husky, yes," she admitted. "But I've never thought anything of it."

"Danny's voice wasn't husky, Jo."

Jo waited.

Alex shifted his position and took a sip of Scotch. "Jo," he said, "there's something you have to believe before I go any further. I fully intended to tell you all about this. There was nothing *wrong* with Danny—" he spoke as if he and the rock singer really were two different persons "—except that he was just a kid and too much came to him too soon. That could have resulted in his making a hell of a mess of his life, and, or, becoming hopelessly spoiled along the way. Thanks to a wonderful guy named Ray Ellerson who Danny— who I—'' Alex hastily corrected himself ''—was lucky enough to get as a manager, that didn't happen.''

"I know I just said there's nothing of Danny Forth in me,'' Alex continued. "That I'm an entirely different person. That's true, more than you might think. But not entirely so. Danny was the young me. What I'm trying to get across is that Danny can never be resurrected. It's not as if I'd simply grown up as Danny Forth, then quit singing at some point and gone on to something else. My life became so altered that I did, in the process, have a total personality change.''

Alex paused. "Does this make sense to you?''

She said slowly, "I think it would make more if I knew what happened to Danny Forth.''

"Well,'' Alex said, his voice sounded hoarser then usual, "one morning, when I was right at the top, I woke up and I couldn't swallow.''

"What?'' Jo asked frowning.

"I'm speaking literally, Jo. I woke up one morning and it was all I could do to swallow. I'd been singing a lot, and I thought maybe I'd strained my vocal cords. I played a concert that night, and by the time the concert was over, it was all I could do to talk at all.''

Again Alex shifted position. "Ray, my manager, insisted I see a throat specialist. I had polyps on my vocal cords.''

"Oh, Alex!'' The cry was wrenched out of Jo.

"I lucked out." Alex said soberly. "They were benign. But the surgery to remove them left some unavoidable permanent damage. So, ever since, I've sounded like...this."

He smiled ruefully. "Needless to say," he said, "I could no longer go on singing. My career was smashed. I was advised, in fact, never to try to sing. I'm fine...but the less I strain my vocal cords the better."

Finally Jo remembered what it was that had nudged her when she'd first realized who Alex was. "There was a story in the paper," she recalled. "Something about you going in the hospital for minor surgery."

"Yes." He nodded. "Ray down-pedaled the situation. The surgery wasn't all that minor."

"But then," she persisted. "I'd swear that I'd read you were fine, about to go back on concert tour again."

"That's true," he agreed. "At least, it's true that you saw the story. There was never a chance of my singing again."

"Ray filtered pieces to the press about how I was taking time off to write some new songs," Alex went on. "You might say, Ray gradually phased me out. It didn't take much doing. Stars fall fast, Jo."

"If your fans had known the whole story..." Jo began.

"That's just it," Alex said. "I didn't want my fans to know the whole story. I could imagine how they'd react. I would have been swamped by their pity...and that was the very last thing I wanted."

Even as he spoke, Alex could feel the waves of sympathy that were emanating from Jo. The last thing he wanted was her pity, especially at this late date.

"Alex, oh God!" she said softly, and Alex winced. "To think I was so critical of your saying you couldn't carry a tune...."

"Is *that* why you turned off the way you did?" Alex demanded.

"Yes. I knew you were lying. Well, maybe lying's a pretty strong word, especially under the circumstances...."

"You don't have to make allowances for the circumstances, Jo. I wasn't lying. I *can't* carry a tune. How can I if I'm not allowed to sing? I had no idea you'd latched on to that statement and that it would be enough for you to make me feel you were about to brush me off."

"Well, I was wrong," Jo acknowledged unhappily. "If I'd only known..."

"What would you have done if you'd only known?" Alex asked her. "Protected me?"

"Alex, there was no question of protecting you," Jo protested. "I wouldn't have leaped to conclusions like I did, that's all." She tried to smile. "My father always said I was too quick to judge," she admitted.

Alex said slowly, "It's not your judgment I'm questioning just now, Jo. It's the way hearing what I've just told you is going to affect you."

"What do you mean?"

"Exactly that. You're looking at me in such a mournful way...."

"Do you expect me to be happy over what you just told me?" Jo interrupted. "Do you think I like the thought you went through so much? I can't imagine that kind of trauma, Alex. Almost overnight, you were forced to give up everything—"

It was his turn to interrupt. "That's just what I'm getting at," he said impatiently. "I don't feel I gave up everything overnight. Far from it. Oh, the initial shock was a blockbuster, I admit that. I went into a funk. But once I found there was no malignancy involved I began to see the other side of the tunnel."

"Ray has a ranch out near Tucson," Alex continued. "We went there together once the doctors gave me the green light. There's something tremendous about the American West. Wide open spaces and a big, big sky and a lot of unspoiled beauty, at least where Ray lives. I needed that."

"It was also a way of making a transition. Of phasing Danny Forth out. Ray fed the press just enough to keep them happy. Less and less, as time went by. Finally, nothing. By then, no one wanted anything."

Jo said softly, "I can't help but think that must have been terrible for you."

"Knowing I could be forgotten so easily? Yes, it was a lesson. I learned a lot about the fickleness of fans, the fickleness of fate. Pretty soon, the same kids were yelling just as loud at other people's concerts. I guess if anything it taught me a lesson in humility I maybe needed to learn."

He paused. "What's important for you to understand, Jo, is that all that's *over*," he stressed.

"Yes, I know it's over."

"Knowing and understanding are two different things sometimes," Alex pointed out. "Jo, I wish you'd make a serious effort to let Danny stay back in the past, where he belongs. I also wish you'd get rid of that tape.''

She said reluctantly, ''Alex, there's no way I could get rid of those tapes. I will agree not to play them again when you're around, though.''

He groaned. ''You're pandering to me when you say that,'' he objected. ''Oh, all right,'' he said, getting up and restlessly pacing over to Jo's picture window, ''I admit I don't like needless reminders. But I can tolerate them if I have to.''

He turned his back to the window and scowled at her. ''God, I wish this had never come up!'' he blurted out. ''I don't want the ghost of Danny between us, can't you see that? Especially since he was your idol when you were a teenager.''

''*You* were my idol when I was a teenager,'' she said gently.

''The hell I was! You didn't know me. What you were seeing on stage was the product of a number of imaginations, including my own. But Ray's, too. And my agents. And whomever I was working for. Nightclub owners. Theater managers. Movie producers. There were a lot of people in my act, Jo. Danny Forth was largely their fabrication. My fabrication, too. But a fabrication. Can you understand that?''

''He—you—came across to me with real feeling,'' Jo insisted stubbornly.

''How do I come across to you now?'' Alex asked abruptly.

''I don't understand why you seem so angry,'' she admitted unhappily.

''Because by dredging up my past, you're muddying up our present.'' Alex broke off. He wanted to tell

her it was their present he was concerned about...
because he'd fallen in love with her. There was no denying his feelings for her. All he had to do was look at
her and all the anger, all the irritation that was brimming started to ebb away. And what he wanted was to
go and put his arms around her, bury his face in her
soft amber hair. Say things in her ear he'd never said
to another woman. And then...

With a firmness born of long discipline, Alex put his
thoughts on hold. It was important to him, more important than he seemed able to convey to Jo, that she
wash any pity she might feel toward him right out of
her system.

He wanted them to meet on even ground, which
would be impossible if one person pitied the other. He
wanted so much for them. But Jo was going to have to
come to terms with what he'd told her before they
could go any further.

Now it was Alex's turn to walk out on Jo. He did it
gently, kissed her good-night, told her he'd call in the
morning. But once he'd closed the door behind him,
it was Jo who sagged and stared at the closed door
disbelievingly.

She went into the kitchen and fixed herself another
vodka and tonic. She felt totally bereft. And hopelessly confused.

Chapter Ten

Jo worked late at the office Thursday. At five-thirty she insisted on Marge leaving and promised she'd be doing so herself shortly. But it was after seven before she walked out and locked the door behind her.

She thought about going to a movie instead of going home. Nothing appealed to her, nor was she hungry.

She pulled into the parking lot at her condo, got out of her car... and then history seemed to be repeating itself.

A tall figure loomed up out of the darkness. Alex said softly, "Well, I was beginning to wonder when you'd ever get here."

"I—I was running late," Jo answered hesitantly.

"Yes, I'd say so. Get caught up on all that paper-work?" There was a teasing note to his voice.

"A lot of it."

Alex lifted up a paper bag, held it in front of her. "I picked up some pasta sauce, all made," he announced. "Now it seems to me you already have the bread and wine on hand. So how about going up to your place so we can see which one of us can cook spaghetti without burning it?"

He tucked his hand through her arm as he spoke, gently and firmly steering her toward the condominium entrance.

Jo didn't know what to say to him. She'd been so *sunk.* Now she couldn't believe he was acting as if they'd set the clock back twenty-four hours.

But having Alex at her side was so wonderful that she wasn't about to start protesting. As they entered her apartment, she was ready to go along with just about any game Alex wanted to play.

Somewhere along his way, he'd acquired two voluminous white aprons. He insisted on tying one around her waist, the other around his. "If we're going to be chefs, we've got to do it right," he proclaimed, then frowned.

"What's the matter?" Jo asked.

"I forgot about getting us a couple of those big white chef hats," Alex admitted.

"Honestly!" Jo protested.

"Honestly," Alex echoed, then reached out and took her in his arms so swiftly that she was caught completely off guard.

"Let's make this a brand-new night, okay, sweetheart?" he asked huskily.

"I'd like that," she managed.

"Jo, this day without you has been eighty-six hours long."

"I know, I know."

"Are you saying you missed me?"

She looked up at him, her smile wry. "How can you ask such a stupid question?"

For answer, his lips descended. Jo stood on tiptoe, reaching for his kiss. She clutched him as their mouths meshed, and her world began to rock around her. Tender at first, his kiss deepened. Then, tantalizingly, he touched the line where her lips met with the very tip of his tongue and gently rubbed back and forth over that spot.

Their lips parted by mutual accord and Jo began to sway slightly, back and forth, still clutching Alex.

His hands moved to her shoulders and began to stroke her with slow, even measures, sculpting her all the way to her waist. Those slow, even strokes were in complete contrast to the way his lips were moving on hers, faster and faster. Then his mouth left hers. His lips ranged heatedly across her chin, then to her ear, where he paused so his tongue could slowly, temptingly, encircle the inner, pearly edge of that ear.

Jo lifted her hands and ran them through his thick dark hair. Her fingers met the back of his head as she instinctively pressed closer to him, felt his arousal, and pressed even closer.

He half carried her to the bedroom. They stood near the window, letting the tropical moonlight spill shards of silver over them as they undressed each other. Alex's fingers were like constant caresses as he took off her clothes. They were possessed of pure magic as they played over her body, inch by inch.

She tugged at his belt, unfastened the buckle, then waited for him to step out of his pants and throw off his shorts. For a long, tantalizing moment they stood apart, eyes searching each other's bodies in the moonlight. Then Alex suddenly swept her up in his arms, carried her to her bed, lowered her....

She knew that he must be as beset by passion as she was, yet he made love to her slowly. Let his hands speak for him, let his mouth continue to express his feelings. She sensed that he wanted this first time for her, especially for her, so she was pliant, letting him proceed at his own pace. Indeed it was she who finally went out of control, sensations spiraling, rising, accelerating, cresting into sunbursts that shattered the surrounding moonlight.

Then, as they lay entwined, she slowly, almost shyly, at first, began her own exploration, tracing the strong muscles that banded his chest and shoulders, gradually discovering the nuances of his body and what her touch did to him. Bringing him to the point where he muttered hoarsely, "Oh God, Jo, I can't hold off much longer...."

And it became the moment for him to enter her. For them to continue together, all the way to the top of the world, then over the edge.

A long time later, Jo and Alex fixed their spaghetti dinner. They sat at Jo's table, which was illuminated by a fat, cream-colored candle, ate and drank wine and stared at each other with stars in their eyes.

Then they made love again. And again, when they awakened in the early hours of the morning. And when finally daylight streamed through the windows, Jo woke up to find she'd pillowed her head against Alex's shoulder and he had an arm thrown over her.

And it seemed to her that was the way it should always be, the way she should wake up every morning.

Alex made coffee and brought a cup to Jo, and she sat up in bed while she drank it. He'd opted to take a shower and came out of the bathroom with a huge, apricot towel wrapped around him. Just the sight of him was enough to knock Jo's props out from under her again.

Alex sat down on the foot of her bed, coffee cup in hand, and suddenly asked, "Jo, is there a chance Greenscapes could do without you for today—and through the weekend as well?"

Before she could answer him he said, "I want to spend every minute with you between now and Sunday night, when I have to fly back to New York. Every minute, sweetheart. I don't even want to miss a single second out of any of those minutes. So . . . take today off, will you?"

Jo tried to recall the appointments she had scheduled. She discovered to her consternation that she couldn't recall much of anything at all, with Alex's imploring eyes upon her. She'd never expected to be in a position where Alex was imploring her about anything, for one thing. Also, business had been uppermost in her mind for so long that it was disconcerting to think that anything or anyone else could preempt it to this extent—even Alex.

She said, "Alex, I'll have to check with Marge."

He didn't attempt to hide his disappointment. He asked, a slight edge to his voice, "What will you do if Marge says there are too many urgent appointments on your calendar for today to erase them?"

Jo sat up a shade straighter. "What would you do, if this were you we were talking about?" she challenged.

He eyed her levelly. "And it was today? Frankly, Jo, I think for once in my life I'd tell business to go to hell."

Maybe, maybe not. He wasn't in that position, Jo reminded herself, so it was easy to say that. But she could imagine that while he was working his way up to becoming such a phenomenal business success, and for much of the time since, Alex would have looked over his daily schedule before he agreed to any outside commitments.

That sounded pretty terrible, she conceded. No one would want to come under the heading of an outside commitment. She wouldn't. Certainly Alex wouldn't. But the point was that although Greenscapes was doing extremely well, she still didn't have Alex's power, wealth and freedom.

A few months from now, she might be in a position to easily accede to a request such as the one he'd just made. But right now...

She became aware that Alex was waiting for her to say something. "Well? What's the verdict?"

Jo had seldom felt more miserable. "Alex," she said, even the words she was speaking hurting her, "I wish I *could* tell my business to go to the devil. But I can't. You have other people, like Andy, you can shift responsibility onto if you want to cut out. I don't. It's not fair to Marge to expect her to juggle around clients to keep them happy. How would you feel if that had happened to you?"

"As I remember, it came very close to happening to me," Alex informed her. "I had the devil of a time even getting you to accept my phone call."

"I had no idea who you were—"

"Or it would have been different, right?"

"Of course it would have been different," she admitted. "Don't you differentiate in your own business? There are only so many hours in the day. You have to do the best you can with them."

"Okay," Alex said evenly. He stood, disappeared into the bathroom again, and Jo leaned back into the pillows, wishing they could suddenly absorb her, wishing she could drop out of sight and recharge for just a few minutes.

She was so used to handling everything herself. Maybe that was her problem, she conceded. On the other hand, she really didn't have anyone with whom to share her load, as she'd told Alex. Maybe Greenscapes should have deferred opening the Miami office and she should have kept Tim here in Sarasota. Maybe she should have thought about adding executive manpower first, before expanding further. She had good people in all the other offices. She had total confidence that Tim would make Miami the kind of operation it should be. But maybe Miami *had* been stretching things a bit too thin.

Jo did a bit of mental calculating and was about to reach for the phone and call Marge when Alex appeared.

He was fully dressed, and he had the look about him of a man on his way out.

He paused at the foot of the bed to say, "I'll call you tonight. Maybe we can have dinner together. Out somewhere."

"Alex—" Jo began.

Alex cut her short. "There's no need for a lot of explanations," he said. "You're right. Just because I've taken a holiday doesn't mean you can. So let's bag today, get together tonight, and make the most of the weekend—if, that is, you'll be free on the weekend."

"I'll be free," Jo mumbled.

"And tonight?"

"Yes."

Alex's gaze softened as he looked at her, and he began to feel slightly ashamed of himself. She *was* right. It was easy for him to talk, when he had people like Andy onto whose shoulders he could shift some of his load, anytime he needed to.

It hadn't always been like that. In the early stages of groping his way around in the business world and then building up Malls International, Ltd., he'd stuck even more strictly to business than Jo was doing now. Of course, no one had come along for whom he'd felt even remotely what he did for Jo. If so, would he have behaved differently?

He had to face up to the answer that no matter how much he might have wanted to, the fact was he probably couldn't have afforded it.

Jo was looking at him with those gorgeous dark eyes of hers as if he'd wounded her.

Alex wasn't often impetuous. But he let himself yield to impulse as he sat down next to her on the bed, reached out, and stroked her amber hair back from her forehead with gentle fingers.

"Sweetheart," he said softly. "I'm sorry."

Tears filled Jo's eyes. And though he'd sworn that women's tears left him unmoved, Jo's tears moved him. He reached into his pocket for a handkerchief, touched it to the tears quivering on her lashes, and said, "You're making me feel like a monster, Jo."

"I—I don't want to make you feel like a monster," Jo said unsteadily.

"Look," Alex said, "go on in to your office. Just cut out as soon as you can, will you? I'll be in my suite at the Floridiana from four o'clock on. Between now and then, I'll latch on to that real estate agent and look at some more property."

Jo reached up, caught his hand in hers and pressed it to her cheek.

"Oh, Alex, Alex, Alex," she murmured. "Sometimes it's hard to know what to do."

"Isn't it, though?" Alex agreed. "But not in this instance. Everything's okay, sweetheart. Believe me." He bent and kissed her lips lightly. "I'll be waiting for your call," he promised.

Jo didn't call Alex. Instead, at four o'clock she knocked on the door of his suite at the Floridiana.

Alex opened the door, stared at her wordlessly, then wrapped his arms around her. He broke away just long enough to glance down at the small flight bag she was carrying.

"Does that say what I think it does?" he asked Jo. She nodded.

Alex scooped her into his embrace again, and the effect of his kiss went clear to her toes. All day long he'd yearned for her. He let that yearning show, without holding anything back.

Jo didn't hold back, either. All day long, *she'd* been regretting her decision to go to work, thinking that the appointments she'd made could have been postponed till the first of the week. By which time Alex would be back in New York, and on the eve of leaving for China.

She hadn't needed Marge to shoo her out of the office early. She'd told Marge, in fact, that she was putting herself out of circulation until nine o'clock Monday morning.

"Now," Marge had answered, "you're getting smart."

Was she? Jo wasn't so sure about that. Spending this weekend with Alex was going to create an involvement so deep there'd be no way she'd be able to extricate herself from it without a lot of heartache. She faced that knowledge. She didn't know what Alex wanted, as far as the future was concerned. In all honesty, she didn't know what she wanted herself. She did know that right now they wanted each other. Could that be enough?

That Friday afternoon they let their honesty and intensity crest between them. They blotted out the world, concentrated on each other, and made love. Passion finally ebbing, they lay on Alex's huge bed, hands clasped, shoulders touching, and talked as daylight merged with the tropical dusk, and then that dusk was transformed into star-studded darkness.

They hadn't been watching the clock, so they didn't know what time it was when they went down for a swim in the Floridiana's lavish pool. They swam almost lazily, mostly side by side. They had no desire for a race, no yearning for competition. That would come again another time. Just now they wanted only the touching, the proximity. They wanted to bask in the revelation that—metaphorically speaking—they were joined.

They showered together. Alex loaned Jo a long white terry robe. Then he ordered supper from room service and fixed drinks while they waited for the food to arrive.

They ate by the window. The reggae band was playing by the pool again. The sensuous tempo had its effect. Neither Alex nor Jo ever finished their late supper. Instead, they went back to bed.

Saturday morning was long, languorous, filled with gentle humor and lazy lovemaking that was almost more provocative than their passion-filled unions of the night before. Then they dressed and went out for lunch at a small seafood restaurant where they indulged in a shrimp feast and made the spur-of-the-moment decision to drive out to Myakka Park.

At the park, they toured Myakka Lake on the old, *Gator Gal* airboat. The captain was a naturalist who fascinated them with his tales of the terrain and description of the flora and fauna that abounded all around them. He was also an expert at flushing alligators. They must have watched at least a hundred of the large reptiles either lazing in the sun along the banks of the lake or else swimming away at the approach of the boat.

They stopped at Jo's condo on their way back from Myakka so she could pick up a couple of changes of clothing. While she was deciding what she wanted to wear, Alex wandered around her living room, admiring the paintings she'd collected and chuckling over her pelican collection.

He'd have to add to that collection, he promised himself. And also reminded himself he had a small present for her he mustn't forget to give her before he left Sarasota. He decided it might be best to treat it as a farewell present.

Farewell. There was a dire ring to the word because it had such finality about it. Alex stirred restlessly, looked out over the sparkling waters of Sarasota Bay, and wondered just where he and Jo were going.

So far they'd been traveling pretty fast. He couldn't relate the few days he'd known her to the depth of his feeling for her. But so much had occurred in those few days. They'd had some honest-to-God spats. Some misunderstandings that easily could have become serious if they hadn't been able to work their way out of them.

Certainly they'd proven that where making love was concerned they were perfect partners. And Alex was fully aware that in giving herself so freely to him, Jo had offered him a great deal. A large share of herself. The thought made him feel strangely humble.

He wanted to be worthy of her; hoped he was worthy of her. He smiled wryly. He still found it difficult to believe that it could always be like this with Jo. Difficult to believe that she might not tire of him eventually and change, and then when he came home one night he'd find she was gone.

He thought of Ray's wise words of counsel. He knew Ray was right and he was wrong. True, a lot of women couldn't be trusted. A lot of *men* couldn't be trusted, either. It was grossly unfair to brand an entire sex because his mother, the first important woman in his life, had left her husband and child and walked out on them without ever bothering to look back.

But it was vastly easier to say that than to accept it. These were gut feelings with him. Gut reactions.

Slender arms stole around Alex's waist. Jo whispered, "A penny, maybe?"

He turned and saw her lovely face looking up at him. "What?" he asked vaguely.

"Okay, a dime? Even a quarter? For your thoughts. You looked so pensive, standing here."

"Pensive?" Alex laughed shortly. "I was just . . . woolgathering," he hedged.

"Lucky sheep."

He grinned, clutched her in a bear hug, and rained kisses on her hair, her forehead. "Lucky sheep, indeed," he muttered.

They left the condo, but as they drove back to the Floridiana Alex felt restless. He needed plain, physical exercise to get himself back on an even keel.

"I feel like a swim, but not in the pool," he confessed to Jo. "How about going over to Siesta Beach and trying out the gulf? Too late in the day, do you think?"

"No, I don't see why it should be."

"So let's get into our suits," Alex suggested.

Jo put on her white bikini and discovered that Alex had also chosen to wear white. His snug-fitting trunks emphasized both his glorious physique and his rich, even tan.

It was late enough in the afternoon to be able to find a parking place at Siesta Beach without too much trouble. They strolled across the white sand hand in hand, left their towels and robes above the tide line, then scampered for the jade-colored water.

The sun was still fairly high in the sky, but it was starting downward. It spilled copper over the shallow waves and Jo said to Alex, "You look like an Aztec god, all bronzed by the sunlight."

"Then you look like an Aztec princess. Have I ever told you how beautiful you are, Jo?"

They were perhaps waist deep in the water, the gentle waves rocking them slightly. Suddenly Jo turned and struck out with long strides, swimming away from him.

He sensed an urgency in her movements and followed, catching up with her in a few long strokes.

"What prompted that great escape?" he asked, turning and floating on his back as he gazed across at her. He spoke lightly, covering up a slight anxiety.

Jo was treading water. She was at an angle from Alex so her face was shadowed. He couldn't read her expression accurately, but it would have been hard not to diagnose pure misery in her voice. "I suddenly remembered tomorrow's Sunday," she said unhappily.

She didn't have to elaborate. Yes, tomorrow was Sunday, and he was booked on an afternoon flight out of Sarasota Airport.

Alex closed his eyes and let the water bear the weight of his body. Twice today he'd nearly told Jo he was having second thoughts about making the China trip himself, and had just about decided to send Andy in his place.

Why hadn't he?

Why didn't he tell her right now he'd change his flight and leave Monday morning, so they could have all Sunday and all Sunday night together?

There wasn't time to think it through. Nor was he able to think that clearly with Jo so close to him. Maybe, once again, it was primarily a gut feeling. In this case, the feeling that both he and Jo were going to need a little space between each other after the intensity of this weekend. A little time to stand on their own feet and do some serious assessment.

Were those excuses on his part? The question nudged, but Alex couldn't answer it; didn't even want to attempt to answer it just now. Instead he flipped over, swam to Jo and kissed her, the salt on his lips blending with the taste of her beautiful mouth.

"We have tonight," Alex reminded her. "And a big chunk of tomorrow. Let's make the most of it, sweetheart."

Chapter Eleven

Sunday morning, Jo and Alex felt a mutual need to get out of his suite. They went down to the pool, swam, and later had brunch on the patio behind the bar. They talked, but again, as if by unspoken consent, they avoided anything really personal.

Then the time came for Jo to drive Alex to the Sarasota airport.

As they parked in the airport lot, a short distance from the terminal, Alex suddenly said, "Oh."

"Forget something?" Jo asked him.

"Nearly." He opened the attaché case propped by his feet and extracted a small box, wrapped in silver and white paper. "For you," he told her.

Jo was sure her pulse skipped several beats. The box looked like a jeweler's box. A box that could contain a ring. Could Alex possibly be giving her a *ring*?

She began to shake inwardly. What was she going to do if she opened this box and found a solitaire diamond blinking up at her? Was she ready for that kind of commitment?

Her heart answered for her mind. *Yes.* She loved Alex Grant. She wanted to spend the rest of her life with him. They had differences, but who didn't? She suddenly felt certain they could work through both their career and personal differences. Juggle, so their lives could come together to form a perfect whole.

Yes. If Alex was giving her a diamond with all that giving a diamond implied, she was going to throw herself into his arms and leave no doubt as to where she stood.

She looked across at Alex. There was a glint of humor in his blue-gray eyes. "Aren't you going to open it?" he queried gently.

Jo's fingers fluttered over the wrappings. She held her breath as she opened the small box. And saw, nestled in cotton, a golden replica of Aladdin's lamp swinging from a slender gold chain.

She kept her eyes lowered, fighting back the stab of disappointment she didn't want him to see.

Alex asked, "Remember? The day of the Mimosa Mall opening? You said you wanted one of the Aladdin's lamps we were giving away. Well, I felt you deserved better than the plastic replicas we were handing out. So I had this made for you by a local jeweler."

"It's lovely," Jo managed to say. The pendant *was* lovely. It was a delicate piece, and the craftsmanship was exquisite.

"May I fasten it on?" Alex asked her.

She shivered as he clasped the gold chain around her neck. Puzzled, he asked, "You're not cold, are you?"

The outside temperature was somewhere in the eighties, yet Jo felt a chill around her heart. Alex was leaving. Neither of them had mentioned the future. So much could happen when paths were separated, and theirs had been joined together so briefly.

Her voice sounded muffled as she murmured, "No."

"Jo?" Alex asked suspiciously. "Hey, you're not crying, are you?"

"I'm trying not to." She struggled to get a grip on herself. Managed to add, "I know how you feel about women and tears."

"No," Alex corrected, "you don't know how I feel about women and tears. Maybe you know how I *felt* about women and tears. But I've been revising some opinions and theories lately."

He didn't elaborate, but glanced at his watch. "Hell," he said dejectedly. "I really do have to go over and check in."

Jo got out of the car. Her legs felt unsteady. She knew if she went into the terminal with him and bade him goodbye at the gate she was probably going to dissolve and shed buckets of tears right in front of him. She didn't want to leave that impression with him as he put Sarasota behind him.

Her voice as unsteady as her legs, she said, "Alex, I'm not too great at goodbyes. So let's just say our *sayonara* here, shall we?"

"I'm lousy at goodbyes," Alex confessed. "The problem is, I don't want to say *sayonara*, *adiós!* or anything else. Jo..."

"Yes?"

"Come to New York with me. Even for a couple of days."

That was the last invitation Jo had expected. As it was, she'd had Marge shift two of Friday afternoon's clients to Monday. With the other business she had booked and paperwork to catch up on she'd be lucky if she got out of her office tomorrow night before dark.

"I wish I could," she said honestly. "But I think you know I can't."

"So much for getting yourself tangled up with a lady executive," Alex commented, with a wry grin.

"I think it's just as frustrating to get tied up with a male executive," Jo retorted promptly.

He laughed. "I had that coming, didn't I? Sweet-heart—kiss me goodbye. Then I'm going to walk to-ward the terminal straight and fast without turning back, or I'll never make it."

She went into his arms. She'd expected a reason-ably gentle goodbye kiss. She didn't get one. His kiss claimed her lips with a repressed savagery that star-tled her. In his way, he was showing her that this part-ing wasn't going to be any easier for him than it was for her.

Maybe there should have been some consolation in that knowing, she thought.

Alex said huskily, "I'll call you tonight."

Jo nodded. Alex turned away, and she didn't watch to see if he'd look around or not. She took him at his word, climbed into her car and drove off. Then, on a whim, instead of going back to her condo she turned in the opposite direction and drove over to Mimosa Mall.

The spacious mall parking lots were filled with cars. Sunday shopping was big in this area, and Mimosa obviously was drawing its full share of the crowd.

Jo entered the mall and tried to pretend she'd never seen it before. She wanted to get as full a "first impression" as she possibly could.

She didn't have to try very hard. The mall plantings were truly beautiful. Jo felt an increasing swell of pride as she strolled through the bazaars, the court-yards, and finally paused in one of the "oases" for a cool drink.

A large replica of Aladdin's lamp hung over the one that was called Aladdin's Court. As she looked at it, Jo fingered the small golden lamp around her own neck. She rubbed it absently, wishing the rubbing would work.

She'd ask the genie to bring Alex back to her.

Alex called that Sunday night. He called again Monday night. He called again Tuesday night. Wednesday, he left for China.

None of the telephone conversations had been sat-isfactory. Alex sounded tired, his voice huskier than usual. But when she expressed concern, he quickly laughed it off.

Jo wished she knew someone with whom she could talk about him. She wished she'd met Ray Ellerson, who she knew was closer to Alex than anyone else, even Andy Carson.

She and Alex had talked over the past week-end...in between making love. He'd given Ray so much of the credit for his current success.

"It was Ray who invested my money for me when I was making it big," he'd confided. "Ray's canny. He consulted the right people and did his own homework as well. After I'd recovered from surgery, Ray went over the facts and figures with me. I could have afforded to be lazy for the rest of my life, if that had been what I wanted."

Jo had smiled at that. "I can't imagine you being lazy for even a month of your life," she'd told him.

"Well," he admitted, "I guess I do have a surplus of energy. Maybe it comes from having had to meet the demands of my first career. It takes enormous energy to be a successful singer. But you're right. Being idle, regardless of money, doesn't appeal to me. I doubt it ever will. Though I wouldn't mind slackening my present pace somewhat...under certain circumstances."

He hadn't spelled them out.

At another moment when Alex had been willing to talk a little bit about his past, he'd confessed that he hadn't gotten his high school diploma until he was twenty-five years old.

"I was out at Ray's place in Arizona," he said. "He told me that with singing closed to me, I needed to start thinking about getting an education. I'd run away when I was sixteen—toward the end of my sophomore year in high school, back in Burlington."

"Did you actually enroll in a school in Arizona?" Jo had asked wonderingly.

"No. Too many people would have recognized me back then. It was still too close to the time when I'd been a star. Ray found a tutor. A man he trusted, so he was sure my cover wouldn't be blown. I worked with this man and thanks to his patience I received a diploma with high honors. After that, via home study, I crammed four years of college into three and then got my bachelor's degree."

"Was that enough for you?"

"No," Alex said. "It might have been enough for me, but it wasn't for Ray. He thought I should go on for a master's in business administration, and I did. By then, I was beginning to explore some new merchandising concepts that eventually led to the founding of Malls International. Everything began to go right." Alex had paused to finish soberly, "I've been very lucky."

Reflecting on that statement during Alex's first week away from her, Jo wondered how many people in his position could have made it. It seemed to her that most people who'd achieved his kind of success in the entertainment field would have been completely wiped out by having that success come to such an abrupt and total end. They would be bitter, no matter what else they might go on to do.

Jo began to understand why Alex didn't want even the memory of Danny Forth resurrected. He'd come to terms with the past, he was his own, strong person in the present. He had no wish to look back.

The trouble was that all through his life—and through both careers—Alex had mostly been a loner, with the exception of his long, close association with

Ray Ellerson. Her problem was that she suspected maybe, deep down inside, he still was.

Jo's phone rang at three o'clock in the morning. She groped for the receiver and heard Alex's husky voice at the other end of the line.

"Sweetheart, I know I'm waking you up," he told her. "But I just couldn't wait to talk to you."

"Where are you?" Jo asked groggily.

She hadn't heard from him for nearly a week and had lost track of where he might be. Andy Carson had called one afternoon to tell her that Alex's stay in China had been extended for a few days. "But he should be back before long," Andy had finished, as if he felt a need to console her.

"I'm in Honolulu." Alex said now, "Ever been here, Jo?"

"No." Jo had done very little traveling outside her native Florida. There had never been time for travel, much though the idea of experiencing faraway places at first hand appealed to her.

"Jo, come over, will you?"

The invitation brushed away the last trace of sleepiness. She sat up, thoroughly alert. "Are you asking me to come to Honolulu, Alex?"

He chuckled. "It's not the end of the world. Book the first flight you can get and you'll be here before you know it."

Jo wanted to groan aloud. Didn't the man have *any* understanding of her work load?

She'd thought they'd been through all that during his last few days in Sarasota. She thought he understood and sympathized with her position. Yet here he was blithely suggesting that she fly off to an exotic paradise, where he could smother her with fragrant leis of gardenias and jasmine and orchids....

Before she could speak, Alex said, "Okay. I know. You can't get away."

It annoyed Jo slightly that he sounded so disgruntled. There he was in his tropical paradise. Here she was, working harder than ever. She asked rather tersely, "How did you happen to stop over in Honolulu? I thought you planned to go straight back to New York."

"While I was still in Beijing I got a phone call from a business connection in Hong Kong," Alex reported casually. "He thought it might be advantageous for me to touch bases with some people here. It's to do with some development on the big island—the island of Hawaii, that is. Though right now I'm here in Honolulu, on Oahu that's to say. I'll be flying over to the big island tomorrow. My thought was that maybe you could join me in Hilo. I have a friend who has a condo there he isn't using. We could take it over for as long as we like. It's in a super locale—"

"Please, Alex," Jo pleaded.

"Please what, sweetheart?"

"Please don't build things up. It's hard enough to refuse you without knowing all those extra, alluring facts."

"I suppose I was hoping if I made enough of a pitch you might reconsider," Alex said ruefully. "Jo, I miss you so much."

"I miss you, too," she told him, her voice breaking on the phrase.

"I want to see you, Jo," he continued, his voice huskier than ever. "Now."

"Alex, you sound so hoarse." Again, she began to worry about him. "Are you?—"

"I'm fine," he cut her off. "The reason I sound the way I do is because I'm choked up from wanting you. I need you, Jo. I need you here. This is a place where we could get away from all the pressures...."

"What about your business deal on the big island?"

"I think I could clear up the details before you even arrived."

"And if you couldn't?"

"What do you mean?" he growled.

"I'm not trying to make a big thing of it," Jo began, "but can't you see what you're saying? You conduct your business...whether in China, Hawaii, or wherever. You give it a definite priority. I don't think you can deny that."

"I'm not trying to deny it."

"Well, I have a business to conduct, too. It just happens to be considerably more centralized than Malls International, that's all. So I don't have the opportunity to go globe-trotting as you do, mixing business and pleasure. As for going globe-trotting for pleasure alone...it's a terrific concept, Alex. But not one I can include in my game plan right now." Her voice broke once more. "Oh, darling," she pleaded, "can't you see that?"

In the silence that followed, Jo became painfully conscious of the miles that stretched between them. Jet age or no jet age, the Hawaiian Islands seemed a long, long way away.

Alex asked huskily, "What have you got on right now?"

"Just a short nightgown," she said. "It's a warm night, but I decided I'd rather sleep without air-conditioning."

"What color is it?"

"Oh, sort of deep peach color."

"Straps?"

"Spaghetti straps."

"Lace?"

"Some."

"Oh, God," Alex moaned, "I'm getting some awfully erotic visions." He sighed. "Sure you won't change your mind about coming over?"

"I can't change my mind," Jo said patiently. And after that the conversation dwindled until Alex said good-night, and she told him where she was it should be good-morning.

The memory of that Hawaiian phone call plagued her all day. In midafternoon, Fred called. "I've gotten down some ideas about the dinner theater complex, Jo. Any time when we could get together so you could look them over?"

Jo was delighted to hear Fred sound so upbeat. And all of a sudden, she couldn't face another lonely evening by herself in her condo.

"How about if I bring out some pizza to your place, and we can go over your sketches this evening?" she suggested.

"Jo, you don't have to bring food with you. Myrna'd have a fit. She's practicing with the kitchen band this afternoon...."

"The kitchen band?"

Fred chuckled. "A bunch of the women have gotten together and they make music with a variety of pots and pans and kitchen utensils. Actually it sounds pretty good. Myrna went off a while ago with a frying pan, a spatula, and something I guess is used for grating vegetables."

"Are they planning to give concert tours?" Jo asked, with a giggle.

"Don't laugh," Fred admonished her. "This is serious stuff. Yes, they're planning to give concerts. I don't think you'll see them appearing at the Van Wezel Hall for a while, but they intend to tour some of the other mobile home parks. Seems they're not alone. Quite a few of the parks have kitchen bands. They're thinking toward a big outdoor, joint concert, maybe next Christmas.

"Anyway," Fred concluded, "Myrna would have a fit if you come out here bringing your dinner with you. Just come, Jo."

"I'll bring dessert," Jo compromised.

Late that afternoon she stopped at a bakery and bought a fresh strawberry pie, and then headed for the mobile home park.

Every inch of the drive reminded her of Alex.

By the time she arrived, she was missing him so much that she felt as if she'd had a permanent ache implanted deep inside her.

This was the first time she'd been out to Fred and Myrna's place since Fred's birthday party but, to her delight, a week ago Fred and Myrna had actually appeared at her Greenscapes office one afternoon. Myrna had gone around the nurseries, looking things over, while Jo and Fred had huddled together in conference just as they had before his illness.

Fred's emotions, she'd been delighted to observe, appeared to be on an even keel again. In fact, Fred looked healthy, alert, and even seemed to be walking better, though he still had to use the cane. Jo had been tremendously pleased, and wished Alex had been around to share her pleasure.

Now she found Fred out in the screened Florida Room that was permanently attached to the side of his mobile home. He'd cleared a big round table, and she could see he was ready to spread out his sketches for her inspection.

Myrna wasn't in sight, but Jo smelled something marvelous. "Fred, is Myrna making her famous beery beef stew?"

"Certainly is," Fred answered promptly. "Minute she heard you were coming, Myrna took off for the store." He beamed. "Jo lady, it's great to see you," he told her affectionately.

Jo hugged him and said, "It's great to see *you*. Especially since each time I've seen you lately you've been looking better and better."

"I've been feeling better and better." Fred nodded. "A lot of it's having an interest to latch onto, Jo. I don't think anyone is ready to be put out to pasture completely, while they still have some use of their brains, and maybe their hands. That's what's happening to too many older Americans, and it's a waste."

Agreeing with him, Jo was gladder than ever that she'd decided to entrust the dinner theater project to him.

Myrna came to the door of the mobile. "What'll it be, folks? Beer, vodka and tonic, or a soft drink?"

"I think I'll go for a vodka and tonic," Jo said, while Fred decided on a beer.

Myrna brought out drinks and some cheese and crackers to munch on, then said, "I'll leave the two of you alone so Fred can show you what he's done, Jo. I know he couldn't possibly wait till after dinner."

Jo saw that Fred's eyes were shining with enthusiasm, and for a second was just a bit disconcerted. Suppose this plantscape of Fred's wasn't up to snuff? It would be very difficult to tell him that, yet she couldn't forget the obligation she owed her client, either.

But Fred's designs were fantastic. He'd captured exactly the mood the theater owner wanted to create. His plans provided a background for a sophisticated restaurant that would still be casual enough to fit a rather laid-back kind of Florida ambience in which people could relax and simply enjoy themselves, while being surrounded by beauty. The plantscape was such that once the stage lights went on and customer attention became focused on what was going on behind the footlights, there would be no visual conflict.

Jo said sincerely, "This is absolutely *great*."

Fred, flushed with pleasure, showed only a second of doubt. "You really mean that, don't you?" he asked Jo.

"Don't you know I mean it?" she challenged him.

He grinned. "Yes," he said. "Yes, I know you so well, Jo. You'd have a difficult time fooling me. Myrna," he called, "come on out. This calls for a real celebration."

They ate at the round table, the sketches having been cleared away and put in a safe place. Myrna's famous stew was as delicious as ever. It was the first thing that had actually tasted good to Jo since Alex had left Sarasota. She surprised herself and delighted Myrna by eating two helpings.

They lingered over the dessert and coffee, while Fred reminisced about some of the early jobs at Greenscapes and some of the mistakes he'd made as a young designer.

The evening passed pleasantly. So pleasantly that Jo hated to leave. The thought of being alone again in her condo had no appeal. Still, she didn't want to keep these two people up past their bedtime.

She was about to say she'd better get on the road when Myrna said, "I nearly forgot. Fred, did you tell Jo about Alex's present?"

Alex's present?

"No, I didn't," Fred admitted. "It came a couple of days ago, Jo. Myrna, get it, will you?"

As Myrna went inside for the present, Jo wondered what Alex could possibly have sent Fred.

"Came airmail from China," Fred announced as Myrna handed him an object which he, in turn, passed to Jo.

Jo found herself looking down at an exquisitely carved jade turtle, and her throat suddenly went dry.

"Alex wrote a note with it," Fred said. "He said that in China the turtle is considered a lucky symbol for health and longevity. Sometimes people rub its back, just for insurance, and he suggested I might give this one a rub now and then."

"Alex also says he hopes he'll be seeing us before much longer," Myrna reported. "He says he's planning to get down here to Florida as soon as he can, to recheck on some property he's been thinking about buying."

Jo tried to mask her surprise—and her sudden feeling that Alex was leaving her out in the cold. He'd said absolutely nothing to her about returning to Sarasota. True, she knew he'd been looking at property on Siesta Key, but she'd more or less put that down to a whim on his part. Often people became struck by a place they visited, and even went so far as to look around at property, thinking they'd like to own a place in the vicinity. But more often than not, once on familiar ground again those plans were never fulfilled.

A few minutes later she said good-night to the Baxters, told Fred to call the office when he was ready to come in and talk to some of the other employees about implementing his designs, then drove off. But as she crossed the bridge over the Manatee and headed toward her condo, she found it hard to concentrate on driving.

Fortunately the traffic was not as heavy as it might have been. As it was, a couple of times irate motorists honked at her, and Jo, her mouth set, realized she'd better pay more attention to what she was doing. All the same, it was hard to shut out a mounting annoyance toward Alex. She supposed it was childish to be miffed about it—actually she was delighted Alex had sent a present to Fred—but he hadn't sent *her* a damned thing!

Much worse, though, was the fact that he'd been divulging his plans to the Baxters, yet hadn't let her in on them.

Maybe she wasn't as important in Alex's scheme as she'd like to think.

Jo didn't sleep too well that night. But in the morning she awoke with a firm resolution.

The next move in this particular game of romantic chess was definitely going to be Alex's.

Chapter Twelve

In early April the weather began to get hot. Most of the "snowbirds" from the North left the area, traffic was lighter, and a more relaxed season for the Floridians, both native and adopted, began. But each morning when she went to work Jo felt less at ease than she had the day before.

There was no word from Alex. That, she diagnosed, was her major problem. She was beginning to think that Alex communicated only when he wanted to do so.

She warned herself that much as she loved him she couldn't let herself be engulfed by him. Which was another way of saying she couldn't sit by idly and wait. Not if she wanted to retain some grip on her sanity.

One morning Jo sat down, made phone calls to each of the branch offices of Greenscapes, Inc., and talked to the person in charge at each of her outlets. By the time she'd finished, she had Tuesday trips scheduled, one per week, to Miami, Tampa, St. Petersburg, Clearwater, Fort Myers and Naples. It was her plan to stay overnight in each of these cities, though they were not so distant that she couldn't easily have managed to complete her safaris in a single day. The excuse she gave herself was that she wanted to become more conversant with the personnel in her branches. Honesty propelled her to add that this would also give her twelve days away from home over the next six weeks or so.

When Jo told Marge what she was planning to do, her secretary raised her eyebrows. "Do you really think it's necessary for you to do that?" Marge asked. "Seems to me you have more than enough to do right here at headquarters."

"Well," Jo hedged, "I've been thinking that I've been lax about checking out the branches. It isn't fair to expect people to run things without ever touching bases with the people from the home office."

"That hasn't exactly been the case," Marge protested mildly. "You know, mountains *can* go to Mohammed. Or should I put it the other way around?"

Jo was scanning a pile of new invoices. "I don't know what you're talking about," she said rather shortly.

"I'm saying the branch managers could come to you if they have a problem, Jo. Oh, I'm not denying it might be a good idea for you to make a personal visit to the different offices now and then. I just don't quite understand why you suddenly feel the need to make regular weekly treks...."

"Because I think it's good business." Jo's retort was even sharper.

"Okay, boss," Marge allowed, with deceptive mildness.

"Marge, book a flight reservation to Miami, will you?" Jo requested. "I'll be going there first. I'll be driving to the other branches, of course. There shouldn't be any problem getting motel reservations, this time of year. But you might make a point of reserving a place for me about a week before each scheduled trip."

"I'll take care of it, Jo," Marge said, this time sounding a bit on the short side herself.

Jo made her first "safari", as Marge insisted on labeling her planned business trips, the following Tuesday. She'd put Miami first on her list because she wanted to see Tim. She just wanted to be with someone dear and familiar to her for a couple of days.

Tim met her at Miami International Airport, and once they'd greeted and hugged each other Jo became aware that her cousin looked slightly perplexed.

"Want to go directly to the office?" he asked her. "Or could I interest you in going over to a place on the beach for lunch first?"

Jo was tired, hot, and actually in no mood for business. What she wanted most was to relax, to forget all about everything... including Alex, who still hadn't gotten in touch with her. It occurred to her that instead of scheduling a group of business trips she should have had the sense to take a week's honest vacation. She should have sought a place far enough off the beaten track so she wouldn't easily be found, but where she could relax and try to put her fragmented act together again.

Alex Grant, she reflected ruefully, had done a real job on her!

"Let's have lunch," she told Tim, sounding a lot terser than she'd intended.

Tim didn't say anything. Not then, or after he'd ensconced her in his small but classy sports car and they'd headed across one of the causeways connecting the City of Miami with the City of Miami Beach. He was silent, in fact, all the way to the luncheon place he'd chosen. A terrace restaurant behind a small hotel, directly overlooking the ocean.

They were given a table shaded by a huge umbrella. Jo sat back, looked out at the vast expanse of the South Atlantic, and muttered, "Endless water."

"What was that?" her cousin asked her.

"Endless water," she repeated. "It goes on forever. At least that's the illusion one gets. I guess nothing really goes on forever."

"Is that supposed to be a profound statement?" Tim queried, a hint of humor finally edging its way into his voice.

Jo was wearing her prescription sunglasses. From behind them, she gave her cousin a sharp look. Tim was tall, thin and good-looking. Where her hair was amber—at least according to Alex—Tim's was coppery. But his eyes were dark like hers. There was a definite family resemblance. A lot of people took them to be brother and sister, and Jo was sure she loved Tim as much as she could ever love a sibling.

She said, "Look, little guy, I don't go around pretending to make profound statements."

Tim was four years younger than herself. She'd started calling him "little guy" when he really had been one. Now the fact that he towered over her made it a humorous nickname.

"Okay, big stuff," Tim rejoined. He eyed her more closely, and the teasing grin on his face began to fade. "All right," he said, suddenly turning very serious. "What is it? What have I done?"

"What have you done?" Jo could not have been more astonished.

"Certainly I've done something," Tim told her, "or you would never have left our home sweet home base to fly over here. Have the customers been complaining about me? Have we been servicing our clients with inferior stock? Or is it something even worse than that? Something so terrible no one has dared whisper a hint of it to me?"

Jo leaned forward. "For heaven's sake, Tim, what are you saying?" she demanded irritably.

"All of a sudden you call up and tell me you're coming over on an inspection visit, and that makes me run a little bit scared...since the edict was issued without warning," Tim told her.

"There was no edict involved," Jo said shortly.

"Not in so many words, no. But why else would you suddenly have decided to descend on Miami like this, cousin mine? The effect's like you wanted to close in quick, so you could put your finger on the problems before I realized you were checking up on me."

Jo sat back, appalled. If Tim had reacted like this to her sudden announcement of a business visit, how were the managers in her other offices going to respond?

Tim, at least, had an edge. He knew her better than anyone else alive, and he could afford to be honest with her. The others, she appreciated, couldn't be that open. After all, she did hold their jobs in her hands. If they resented her actions as much as Tim evidently did, the chances were they would try to camouflage it. Which would only make the situation all the worse.

"I don't know why you're looking at me like I suddenly pulled the rug out from under your feet, Jo," Tim said. "I'd say that's your strategy at the moment, not mine. Except that I can't think of any reason why any rugs need to be pulled out in the Miami office. In my humble estimation, we've been doing fine. So what's the gripe?"

"There isn't any gripe, Tim," Jo said bleakly.

"Then if you wanted to trek over to Miami just to see my smiling face, why didn't you say so?"

"Because I didn't," Jo fumbled. "Oh, I wanted to see you, it isn't that. But you see . . ." She hesitated.

He waited.

"Well, I got this idea that I should touch bases personally with all the offices. Make it a habit to tour around now and then. My thought was to give a little moral support and familiarize myself with the scope of the whole Greenscapes operation. Not to criticize."

Tim leaned back, his dark eyes scanning her face. Watching his appraisal, Jo began to feel uncomfortable. Tim knew her very well. And, she recalled, had possessed the uncanny ability to be able to see through her, ever since they were kids.

"Jo," he said, "this wasn't just a case of your suddenly feeling slightly stir-crazy, was it? I mean, you didn't happen to wake up one morning and decide you had to start making plans to get out of Sarasota now and again, did you?''

"Damn it!" Jo exclaimed. "Why do you always have to hit the nail on the head?''

Her cousin laughed. "You do the same thing with me," he reminded her. "Remember when I was in love with that lovely Yankee from Delaware last year? You said I was just a winter romance for her. I didn't speak to you for nearly a week. But boy, were you ever right.''

Jo flinched. She remembered the girl in question very well. Female intuition, by whatever name, had raised warning flags when Jo saw her with Tim. Attractive though Tim was, this girl came from a wealthy Northern family and was quite involved in the social whirl back in Wilmington. Jo had felt certain she wouldn't give up her life-style and move to Florida for the sake of a permanent relationship with Tim.

When she'd been proved right, she'd experienced no sense of victory. She knew Tim had been hurting.

But Tim had recovered. He said now, "Don't look so stricken. It was a good thing it happened the way it did. Diane wasn't cut out to be a Florida nurseryman's wife. And I certainly could never have made the transition to her turf.''

Jo heard Tim's words and felt a little bit sick. They applied too precisely to the situation between Alex and herself—with the sex roles reversed. Any permanent relationship with Alex would mean giving up Greenscapes, she felt certain of that. And she couldn't. Much as she loved Alex, Greenscapes was in her blood. She would feel incomplete without her work.

It wasn't as if she could solve the situation by getting a job with another company that essentially did the same thing, somewhere closer to Alex's home base. She was used to running her *own* company. It made a big difference.

Bitterly she reminded herself that Alex hadn't made any offers, anyway. Quite the opposite, in fact. What he seemed to want was an occasional rendezvous in places like New York or Honolulu.

She became aware that Tim was regarding her closely. Gently he asked, "Just what is the problem, Jo?" Want to tell?"

Jo shook her head. "No."

"Then let me guess. A man?"

"Yes."

"Don't tell me there's a man in the world dense enough to resist your charms," Tim teased, but there was a worried look in his eyes.

"It's not a question of...of resistance," Jo said lamely. "Tim, if I could talk to anyone about it, it would be to you. Right now, I just...can't."

"I understand," Tim said gravely. "There was a time when I couldn't talk about Diane, either. But that's long over. The wound has healed. And I love women just as much as ever," he added with a smile. "What I'm saying, Jo, is that you mustn't let whoever he is throw you. If it's right, it'll work out. Which-ever...whenever you want a shoulder, I can offer a choice of two sturdy ones."

"Thanks," Jo said, and was afraid if Tim kept on this way her emotions would start getting ragged again, as they tended to do too often of late.

She forced her mind back to business. "Tim," she said seriously. "Do you really think these field trips are a mistake?"

"No," he reassured her. "It's not the idea of your wanting to take trips around the different offices. It's the way you've gone about doing it, Jo—like you were intending to lower a boom. At least, that's the way your announcement struck me. So I can only assume it may have had even more of an effect on your other managers. They might really start running scared if everything wasn't a hundred percent."

Tim shrugged. "From what I observed when I was at headquarters, I'd say while our branches may not operate at full efficiency all the time, they come pretty close to it. So it's sort of too bad to rock the ship. See what I mean?"

"Yes, I see what you mean," Jo muttered uncomfortably. She frowned. "What should I do, Tim? Cancel the other visits?"

He shook his head. "Definitely not," he told her. "What I would do, though, is to make an advance phone call to each of the managers, a couple of days before your visit is scheduled. Keep a light touch. Just tell them that this was something you made up your mind to do on the spur of the moment, and if you came on strong you didn't intend to. Let them know that you're pleased with their performance—unless you have reason not to be—and emphasize that you think the field trips will do *you* some good. Tell them you think the overview tends to be rather narrow when you stay at headquarters all the time. Which happens to be true."

Jo leaned back and smiled tremulously at her cousin. "Thanks, Tim," she said gratefully. She sighed. "Don't know what I'd do without you."

"You'd manage very well, Coz, much though it may hurt my ego to tell you that," Tim said, giving her the benefit of his infectious grin. "You're a survivor, Jo."

Jo thought about that statement of Tim's a couple of days later on the way back to Sarasota. Was she a survivor? Could she keep going by herself, no matter what?

By "no matter what," she meant if she and Alex were going to part. Could she survive without becoming both brittle and bitter?

That familiar, intense longing for Alex swept over her, in its way answering her question. She missed him so much.

It was only an hour's flight from Miami, so it was early afternoon when Jo arrived in Sarasota. She'd left her car at the airport, and decided to go right to the office.

The first words Marge said to her were, "Alex Grant has been trying to get you."

Jo paused in her study of the mail that had arrived in her absence. "When?" she asked.

"Well, I think the first call came about an hour after you left here. I didn't know what to do, Jo. I was tempted to tell him he'd be able to reach you in Miami. But...I sort of got the idea you were trying to get away from...well, maybe from Alex, as well as from a lot of other things."

"What did you tell him?" Jo asked tersely.

"I said you were away on business," Marge reported unhappily. "Jo, did I make a mistake? He called about every two hours until yesterday afternoon. That's when he was leaving."

"Leaving?" Jo's voice was sharp. "Leaving for where?"

"Sweden, I believe. He said he planned to be in Stockholm for about a week."

"Did he leave a number?"

"No. Jo..."

"It's okay, Marge, really it is," Jo consoled her secretary. "If Alex wants to get in touch he'll try again."

Alex didn't immediately try again, however. But the following week, when Jo returned from a trip to the Tampa office, history repeated itself.

She walked into her office feeling pretty triumphant, because—having followed Tim's advice and paved the way more diplomatically—the Tampa trip had been a decided success. She'd had a chance to touch bases with both the manager and his assistant, and had discovered that the assistant manager had a real interest in spending some time at the Sarasota headquarters, learning the business more thoroughly.

On the flight back, she'd done some thinking about shifting personnel occasionally for greater overall benefit. It would be a good idea to bring in people from the branch offices to work at headquarters—say, for six-month periods—on a rotating basis. They would leave with a much more thorough grounding both in the nursery business and in floral design. Subsequently they'd be that much more valuable to the firm, and she'd make it well worth their while, via an incentive program, to stay with Greenscapes.

Having managerial personnel on that level at headquarters would also give her considerably more freedom than she had now, Jo reckoned. She knew she still had a couple of lessons to learn about business. One was to manage the delegation of authority better. Thus far, she hadn't really had anyone to delegate authority to. With this program, she would always have a right-hand man on hand. And she'd be giving other people a chance.

She had to admit to herself that since her father's death she'd been somewhat jealous about running the whole show herself. A good part of that was because she'd wanted so desperately to fulfill her father's dream and keep building Greenscapes toward the kind of success if was presently enjoying. But the moment had come to loosen the reins a little—not only for her own sake.

As she walked into her office, she was thinking that she'd call the Tampa manager the next day and find out how he felt about her "robbing" him of his assistant manager for six months. She was sure he'd be receptive. He was that kind of person.

Then she looked at Marge and groaned. "Not again?" she asked.

"Again." Marge nodded.

"And where is Alex now?"

"He's been calling from Stockholm, but he was leaving there yesterday for Vienna. Something about a mall in an area where there are a lot of vineyards. He said to tell you he'd had the romantic notion of suggesting you join him in Vienna so the two of you could do some wine tasting.''

"He *knows* I can't do things like that," Jo said testily.

"I don't know," Marge said. "I think if I were you, maybe I'd take him up on one of those trips. Otherwise..."

Jo's mouth tightened. "Are you suggesting that otherwise I might lose him altogether?" she inquired.

"Jo, that's not for me to say. But I think that Alex is..."

"Yes?"

"Well, I think he's a very lonely man," Marge said.

Jo stared at her secretary as if she'd suddenly lost her mind. "Marge, what are you thinking of?" she chided. "Alex *lonely*?" She shook her head. "How could he be lonely? He's handsome, he's rich, he's self-confident, charming..."

"I know," Marge insisted stubbornly. "But I still think he's a very lonely man."

They were in Marge's office, which also served as a reception room. Impulsively, Jo pulled a chair up next to Marge's desk and sat down. "Why?" she asked.

"You can't always put words to feelings like that," Marge said hesitantly. "But... there's just something about him, that's all. I'd say that for all of his outward charm he's a very private person. Sometimes, when he doesn't think you're watching him, the look in his eyes gives him away. Like at Fred's party..."

"Yes?" Jo prodded.

"Well, he looked like a kid with his face pressed against a candy store window. Looking at all the goodies he couldn't have. Like he was seeing something he wished he had, but he knew he was on the outside.''

"Marge," Jo said gently, "don't you think it's a bit absurd to imagine that Alex would envy people living out there? He could buy and sell the whole park if he wanted to."

"Maybe," Marge agreed, "but that's not what I'm talking about. Those are real people, and I think Alex enjoyed being with them. I think he also saw a kind of, well, I guess you'd call it a kind of caring that maybe he doesn't get much of himself. Oh," she admitted, "I may be way off base, Jo."

"I don't know whether you are or not," Jo said frankly.

Later, alone in her own office, she couldn't get the things Marge had said off her mind. Marge was a warm and caring person. She, her husband, and their two sons were very close. Usually she was very intuitive about how other people were really feeling.

Still…Alex *lonely*? Jo smiled wryly. *She* was lonely. She'd spent a large chunk of her time being lonely since her father's death. But she'd been so busy that she hadn't had the time to brood much about it. And she'd almost gotten used to having loneliness as a companion.

She'd learned, too, that loneliness didn't necessarily mean being alone. You could be at a party in a room full of people, and still be lonely.

Was Marge right?

Jo closed her eyes, and willed the phone to ring. She even indulged in the purely superstitious gesture of stroking the little Aladdin's lamp she always wore around her neck and silently commanding the genie to appear. But nothing happened.

Alex called a week later.

"Don't tell me you've finally decided to stay put for a while," he said, as soon as he and Jo had been connected.

She snorted. "You're one to talk! Where are you now?"

"In New York. I got in from Vienna yesterday, and I don't think I've ever had a worse case of jet lag."

"Well, I should imagine you're at the top of the roster in the million-mile flyers' club, or whatever they call it," Jo said dryly.

"You could have put in a few miles yourself if you'd agreed to meet me in Vienna," he pointed out.

"I couldn't meet you in Vienna."

"Business, business, eh?"

"Again, who's talking? Are you going to be in New York a while?"

"If I stayed here, would you come up?" he asked immediately.

Bruce Chapman, the assistant manager from Tampa who was going to be at the Sarasota headquarters for the next six months, was scheduled to arrive the following day. Jo sighed. There was no way she could possibly walk off and leave Bruce before he even knew what was expected of him in his new job.

Alex heard the sigh and said, "I suppose the answer is no."

"Yes, I'm afraid the answer has to be no," Jo admitted. She hesitated, then ventured, "Quite some time ago, the Baxters mentioned you'd told them you planned to come down here again. As a matter of fact, I'd rather expected to see you here before now.''

"That *had been* my intention," Alex admitted. ''It just hasn't been possible, that's all.''

As he said that, he knew it was essentially true...but not entirely. He *could* have sent Andy off on some of these trips he'd been making lately, even though in each case his own presence had been requested.

He supposed he could have snatched a couple of days along the line to get down to Sarasota, too. But he'd feared that such a fleeting visit might do more harm than good. He'd come to the conclusion that time away from each other would give them each the chance to regroup—to think about the transition from Step One to Step Two.

Jo asked, ''Are you still there, Alex?''

"Yes, I'm sorry," Alex said quickly.

"So am I," Jo answered him. ''I wish I could come to New York. Right now I just can't. I'm trying out something new in the business—''

"Jo, you don't have to explain to me.''

"I want to explain to you, Alex. I want you to know that...that if I could possibly manage it, I'd join you in New York.''

Alex tried to lighten the atmosphere. ''In other words," he teased, ''you want a rendezvous?''

But Jo's voice broke as she asked, ''Don't you know how much I want to see you?''

"The first part of June I have to be in Puerto Rico," Alex went on. ''Suppose I get right down to business, and on the weekend you plan to fly to San Juan and meet me? Just for the weekend. That's all I'm asking.''

This time around, Jo wasn't about to say no.

Chapter Thirteen

It was even hotter and more sultry in San Juan than in Sarasota. But when Jo saw Alex standing in the Arrivals section of the airport the weather ceased to matter.

She walked toward him carrying her purse and a tote bag, and stopped short when she saw him staring at her disbelievingly. "I can't believe I'm seeing you," he said, his husky voice if anything a shade huskier. "I was wondering whether you were really going to turn up."

For a second it hurt to think he had so little faith in her. Then even that ceased to matter, because Alex was *here* and so was she, and as he held out his arms she went into them.

She dropped everything as he embraced her, conscious only of him. She didn't know whether she kissed him or he kissed her. It didn't matter. Their kiss fused, their lips clung. And Jo didn't know how she had managed to live without him through all those weeks of spring and early summer.

While she waited to claim the single suitcase she'd brought, Alex went to get his rental car and told her he'd be just outside the airport's main entrance. So, as she stood there alone, Jo finally focused on where she was—and became conscious of the crowd, the confusion and the incessant babble of fast-spoken Spanish.

She'd studied Spanish for a couple of years in high school, and had taken a year of it in college. But as she listened now, she doubted her school Spanish was going to do her much good.

Finally, clutching her suitcase, Jo followed the crowd to the main waiting room and found the front entrance. At once she spotted Alex. He'd rented a small, bright red compact car.

Jo snuggled into the front seat next to him and, as he drove, feasted her eyes on his profile. Was it just her imagination that he looked tired, strained? Maybe she just wanted to think he'd been having as bad a time getting along without her as she'd had getting along without him.

Alex had booked a suite in a hotel in the Condado, San Juan's glittering tourist section. Each room had a huge picture window that looked out directly on a beach where the sand was a deep tan. Dark rocks formed a breakwater on one side, and Jo saw that there were people lying out in the glaring sun on over-size beach towels, using the rocks for partial shadow.

As she gazed out the window, Alex came up behind her, slid his arms around her waist and pressed her close. She closed her eyes, welcoming his embrace. But at the same time she wondered why she was feeling so tense.

He apparently felt it, too, for he automatically stepped back, releasing his hold on her. That wasn't what Jo wanted, yet she felt powerless to do anything about it. Her reflexes might as well have been frozen along with her responses. Now that she was with Alex again, she just didn't seem to be able to function.

He suggested huskily, "Why don't we cut out for a while and let me show you some of the local atmosphere . . . starting with a piña colada down in the cocktail lounge?"

Jo nodded, not knowing what to say to him. Although their initial kiss on meeting had been ecstatic enough, now that they were alone everything seemed different.

They were silent on their way down in the hotel elevator. There were quite a few people in the cocktail lounge, which spilled out onto a terrace overlooking the sea. At the opposite end of the lounge, the gate that led into the casino had just been opened. There were some early luck-seekers playing the slot machines, while a few more ardent gamblers were beginning to fill the blackjack and roulette tables.

"Want to try your luck before we settle down for a drink?" Alex asked Jo, gesturing toward the casino.

"I've never gambled," she admitted.

"Are you against it?"

"Well, compulsive gambling, yes. But I've never really been anywhere before where gambling was legal."

He chuckled. "Then let me get you a few house dollars," he offered, "while you pick out one of the slots that looks good to you. Maybe you'll hit the jackpot."

There were several rows of glittering slot machines, and Jo settled on one nearby. Following Alex's instructions, she dropped a dollar into the slot and pulled the handle. Cherries, lemons, plums and oranges whirled around, and when the machine finally ground to a stop, she saw that her chosen row had come up with an orange, flanked by two lemons.

"Afraid you wiped out," Alex told her.

Jo tried again, and this time came up with a combination of lemons with a single gold bell. By the third try she was muttering, "I think this is a waste of money. Here, Alex. Take back the rest of your dollars and see what you can do with them."

Alex shook his head. "Not just now," he said, pocketing the coins Jo handed him. "I don't think the vibes are right."

The statement sank in. He was referring to the slot machines, of course, but Jo had the unhappy feeling that the vibes between the two of them weren't right, either.

What had happened? Had there been too much time and space between them? Had they lost the magic that had been such a potent force?

"Want to have a drink indoors, or out on the terrace?" Alex asked.

"I think I'd like to go out to the terrace," Jo decided.

A smiling waiter brought the frosty piña coladas Alex had ordered. Jo's throat was parched, and the drink both felt good and tasted delicious. It was bright on the terrace. She reached for her sunglasses and slipped them on, and was glad not only for the way they filtered the dazzling light but for the camouflage they furnished. Her eyes too often gave her away.

Alex slipped on sunglasses, too. Then he said, "There's a pool with its own outside bar on the other side of the hotel. Maybe you'd like a sunset swim? Or we could try out the ocean, for that matter."

Jo stirred restlessly. "I don't know," she murmured.

"Sweetheart..."

Jo looked up swiftly as Alex spoke. He'd so often called her that. She listened as he said gently, "I know. I'm feeling strange too, Jo. But, I think it's natural. Back in Sarasota, I thought what we both needed was some time away from each other. Now I'm beginning to believe I may have been wrong. Maybe we should have stayed together and worked things out...."

"Could we have?" It was a question Jo was almost afraid to ask.

"I don't know," Alex admitted. He smiled faintly. "We have one quality in common, and it's not an easy one to deal with."

"What?"

"We can both be stubborn as hell."

"But I haven't been that stubborn with you," Jo stated self-righteously.

"Haven't you? I'd say if you weren't stubborn," Alex said, with no rancor in his tone, "you would have come to Honolulu. And to New York. And to Vienna."

"You know I couldn't just drop everything and leave my business," Jo reminded him.

"Couldn't is a big word," Alex observed. "Where there's a will there's a way."

"Are you saying you think I didn't *want* to meet you?"

"Perhaps."

"Alex..." Jo hesitated. She didn't know how to explain this to him. "I can't remember," she said finally, trying to choose the right words as she went, "when I've ever felt myself a completely free agent. That's to say, able to come and go as I chose. Even when I was in college, I used to help Dad out on all my vacations. So I just never went gallivanting around like a lot of the others in my class, or got summer jobs in different places." Jo paused.

"Then," she said, "Dad was sick for quite a long time before he died. Tim—my cousin, who heads our Miami office—was around a lot then, though he was still in grade school part of the time. When he was with us, though, I could rely on him. It was a big help.

"Then, well, Dad died, and the whole business fell on my shoulders...."

"Did it *fall* on your shoulders, Jo, or did you just assume the load?" Alex asked her.

After a moment's reflection, she said thoughtfully, "Both, I guess."

"Do you admit that there was a certain ego trip involved in handling the whole show?" Alex queried.

She glanced at him suspiciously. "What are you getting at?"

"Jo," Alex said gently, "I've been the whole route, don't you see? I've taken my share of power trips."

"I do not take power trips," Jo denied hotly.

"I'm not saying there's anything wrong with it, sweetheart. We all need to have our feathers stroked now and then."

"Well," Jo said frankly, "you're certainly ruffling mine, if that's what you wanted to do. But—"

"I don't mean to, Jo," Alex said patiently. "I'm just trying to make you see that your business has grown too big for you to handle on your own. That's what happened with Malls International...."

"Greenscapes isn't even in the same league as your business," Jo interrupted. "You know that."

"Not in size," Alex conceded. "But the basics are the same. I would never tell you *not* to stay at the helm," he went on. "You need to remain in charge, and to know you're up-to-date on everything that's going on within your corporation. But you've also got to build up a backlog of employees you can trust. Suppose, God forbid, you got sick and suddenly had to have emergency surgery?"

"Well...if something like that happened, I'd bring Tim in from Miami," Jo declared.

"Suppose for some reason Tim couldn't leave Miami. Can't you see that you need more than one trusted employee?" Alex urged her.

"I have a lot of trusted employees," Jo snapped.

"I'm sure you do. But not at a chief executive level."

"How many chief executives does a firm need, Alex?"

"A firm needs enough executive personnel so the gaps will be filled if the boss has to step out for a while," Alex told her. "Believe me, it was a long time before I could see that myself. Until I *did* finally come to see it, I was a slave to my own business. It's my own experience that's making me point this out to you now, Jo," he added. "I think sometimes one tends to become as jealous of one's business as of a child or . . . a lover."

"You think I'm jealous about Greenscapes?"

"Jo, I'm not making any accusations." Alex paused, noting her empty glass. "Another drink?" he suggested.

"No, thanks. I think maybe I'd like to walk for a while," Jo said. Somehow she still felt restless.

"Window-shopping along the Condado, or a stroll along the beach?" Alex asked. Mentally he berated himself for pursuing a subject she was obviously so loath to discuss. Why had he brought it up *now?*

"Along the beach."

They strolled down to the shore. Jo slipped off her sandals and after a moment Alex took off his loafers.

The descending sun was at their backs. Just the opposite of the way it had been when they were on Siesta Beach, Jo reflected, and felt a sudden pang of homesickness for Florida.

She felt a lot more in command when she was on her native turf, more secure in both her business and personal relations. Ever since she'd met Alex at the airport this afternoon she'd been floundering.

She said suddenly, "I *have* initiated a few of the things you've been talking about at Greenscapes."

Alex was watching a young boy and a girl tossing a beach ball back and forth. They were doing so at a leisurely tempo, and there was a seductiveness in the way the big orange and red ball floated from one to the other. There was a feminine grace about the girl as she swooped to retrieve it, and a lithe masculinity about the boy as he tossed it back to her. In its own way, it was a courting game.

Ever since Jo's plane had landed that afternoon, all *he* and the woman he loved so deeply had done was quibble—and about business, to boot. They needed to switch to a courting game!

Why had he gotten into all this garbage about the proper running of a successful business? Well, it wasn't garbage, he conceded. What he'd been saying was true enough. But this was neither the time nor the place to have said it.

He felt more than a bit ashamed. The truth was that it still nettled him to think she didn't fly to Hawaii to spend a few glorious days with him, business be damned. Nor had she come to New York, never mind Vienna. There they could have wandered along the Kärntnerstrasse together, have gone out to Grinzing to sample the new wine, and whirled high over the city in the enormous big red Ferris wheel in the Prater.

He'd told himself that if Jo really loved him half as much as he loved her, she wouldn't have been able to resist his invitations. But she'd turned him down as easily and as firmly as if she were turning down a chance invitation from a casual friend.

Brooding about that, it occurred to Alex that Jo had never said she loved him.

Alex took Jo to dinner that night at a beautiful Spanish restaurant in the heart of Old San Juan, the original, Latin sector of the city that was a total contrast to the modern, far more Americanized Condado area.

The dark-eyed Castilian waiters, the delicious food and the soft Spanish music played by a combo in the background, prompted Jo to comment, "I feel like we're in Madrid, even though I've never been there."

"We could be." Alex nodded. "Or maybe Seville."

He almost added, "One day I'm going to show you all those places," but he held the words back. The way things were going, he didn't want to peer very far into the future.

The atmosphere in the restaurant, with its stark white walls, dark furniture, soft candlelight and beautiful flowers was as romantic as anything possibly could be. Yet Jo began to discuss business again over their *tapas*—a selection of succulent appetizers.

"I've brought a man from the Tampa office to headquarters," she told Alex, as she speared a shrimp that had been delicately sautéed in olive oil and herbs with just a hint of garlic.

"Oh?" Alex queried politely. He honestly didn't want to talk about business anymore. Damn it, before this night was over he wanted to be making love to her. He wanted to be with her, enjoy her company, *show* her his love. Sharing this evening with her was more important now than any of their other times together. They had to recover lost ground, and then progress from there. Didn't she understand that?

He watched Jo take a sip of sherry, and listened with mounting impatience as she went on, "When I was in Tampa recently, I was impressed by Bruce Chapman, the assistant manager of our office there...."

Alex perked up his ears. In what way had she been impressed by Chapman?

"It was getting to know Bruce that made me see how I could work out a plan to gradually develop key personnel to a top executive level," Jo continued.

It took all of Alex's willpower to refrain from tapping his fingers on the table or letting his right foot start to keep time with the tempo of the music. Whatever had Jo turned into since he'd last been with her? A high-powered business machine?

Jo didn't look like a business machine of any kind, he admitted wryly. She'd never looked more beautiful than she did tonight. She was wearing a dress that was soft, draped, yet at the same time clingy, so her figure was delineated in an entrancing way. She wore gold earrings—but he felt a stab of disappointment when he didn't see the little gold Aladdin's lamp he'd given her. The slender column of her neck was bare.

"Bruce is going to be with me for six months," she went on, and Alex became aware that he'd lost at least a few sentences of what she'd been saying to him. "Then I think I may put him in one of the branch offices, in the managerial slot, so that I can move that manager to headquarters for what I suppose you could call advanced executive training. Then—"

Jo paused, noticing Alex's silence. He appeared to be gazing at a spot somewhere over her head. So she cut her account short and finished, "You can see what I'm trying to do."

"No," Alex corrected her, and she heard a decided edge to his voice. "I don't see what you're trying to do."

"Well, what you've been telling me about the value of properly delegating authority is right, and that's what I've been learning," Jo said seriously. "Maybe I have been jealous about my own slot at Greenscapes. But even before our talk this afternoon I'd come to realize that I need experienced, reliable, backup personnel on the executive level. So—"

"So, will you kindly shut up?" Alex asked her, keeping his husky voice so low that it could not possibly be heard beyond their table.

Jo was staggered. She'd almost come to the conclusion that business was the one thing the two of them could safely talk about. She'd taken it for granted that Alex had an almost unlimited interest in business, and enjoyed the chance both to play devil's advocate and to give her the benefit of advice gleaned from his greater experience.

She sat back, shocked, feeling as if he'd slapped her in the face.

Alex mumbled apologetically, "I'm sorry. But if you don't get off it, I think I'm going to go crazy. My God, Jo, is Greenscapes all you ever think about?"

Jo choked back a bitter laugh. Was Greenscapes the only thing she ever thought about? She felt like snarling that sometimes she had the devil of a time thinking about her business at all, because thoughts of *him* kept intervening. She couldn't remember the night in recent weeks when his face hadn't swum before her eyes as she was trying to get to sleep, arousing feelings that more often than not had kept her awake into the small hours.

Alex had in fact a tendency to pop up in her mind and usurp her vision at the most unexpected moments. Sometimes—like the other day, when she'd been lunching with a client—she'd see someone with thick, smooth dark hair like his and her heart would do a somersault. Or she'd be at the beach and spy a tall, bronzed, dark-haired man, and suddenly a wave of feeling would come over her of such proportions that she felt herself, emotionally speaking, being swept out to sea.

One thing Jo had learned these past few weeks was the power of concentration. She'd always thought she had a great deal of discipline when it came to focusing entirely on her business affairs, but Alex had undermined even that. Sometimes it took every atom in her to build up enough resolve to give her complete attention to something really important to Greenscapes—but the thought of Alex was always lurking right around the corner.

She knew he was still miffed because she hadn't flown off to meet him before. Part of the reason why she'd been babbling so much about Greenscapes was that she wanted him to understand—a lot better than he seemed to—why she just wasn't as free an agent as he was.

She'd thought that he would have been satisfied because she *had* taken off now and come here to Puerto Rico when he'd asked her to. Wasn't that enough?

"Jo!" Alex said urgently.

"What?" She was still dazed by what she saw as his rudeness.

"Look, I'm sorry. But can't you see I don't want to talk business? I just want to be with you. I've missed you so ungodly much. Haven't you missed me at all?"

"Of course I've missed you," Jo said unsteadily.

"Then, sweetheart, can't we try to...to get back some of the magic we shared?" Alex asked her. "I don't know how, but we have to. After all," he finished, "we only have tonight and tomorrow."

We only have tonight and tomorrow.

Just what, exactly, did Alex mean by that?

Chapter Fourteen

They parted at the San Juan airport. Alex was flying back to New York. Jo's flight was nonstop to Miami, where she'd pick up a connecting plane for Sarasota.

Alex solemnly kissed her goodbye. "I'll call you from New York tonight," he promised, then turned away to head for the gate from which his plane was scheduled to depart, ten minutes earlier than hers.

Jo watched his retreating back feeling as though she was holding back gallons of tears, yet she was dry-eyed. *Maybe when you have too many tears to cry, they're bottled up somewhere and never reach your eyes,* she thought. Certainly she'd shed her share of inward tears over the weekend in San Juan. And she wished, bitterly, that she'd never agreed to this rendezvous.

Last night she and Alex had taxied from Old San Juan back to their hotel. Then, as if neither of them wanted to face up to being alone in the suite, they hadn't entered the hotel but instead, had strolled along the Condado. Most of the shops stayed open late. Jo was surprised to see the golden arches of McDonald's, as well as a Dunkin' Donuts, several other fast-food outlets and a couple of chain pharmacies among the small boutiques and souvenir stores.

She bought a few postcards of both the Condado section and Old San Juan, not with the thought of sending them to anyone but, rather, to keep as a *recuerdo* of this place for herself. She liked what she'd seen of Puerto Rico, and knew she was only touching the tip of the iceberg by visiting San Juan. *Maybe some day,* she thought, *I'll be able to come back and stay a while.*

She bought some jewelry for Marge and Myrna, and a couple of the cool, embroidered cotton Guayabera shirts, favored so much by the local men, for Fred and Len.

She saw nothing that she thought would be suitable as a remembrance gift for Alex. Evidently he felt the same way, because he didn't ask her if she'd like to have any of the things she was looking at, and made no purchases of his own.

Back at the hotel, Alex suggested once more that they try their luck in the casino. Jo was tired and she really didn't want to gamble because it was something of which she'd had absolutely no experience. But Alex insisted on staking some chips for her and they took their places at a roulette table where, in a remarkably short length of time, Jo lost the whole stake.

Alex wasn't much luckier. He won on a couple of turns of the wheel, but soon was wiped out himself. Jo was afraid he might return to the cashier's window for more chips, but he finally said reluctantly, "I guess this just isn't our night," and let it go at that.

It wasn't their night. Though they both tried hard to recapture some of the former magic once they were alone in the suite, that magic proved to be elusive. They made love, and though Alex was tender and considerate, the kind of passion she remembered just didn't crest as it had done before. She lay awake after Alex had drifted into sleep, feeling restless, dissatisfied, and somehow to blame for it all.

Where had she gone wrong?

Sunday they had a late breakfast and then Alex made arrangements with the concierge in the hotel to rent a taxi with an English-speaking driver, so they could have a personalized tour of San Juan.

They visited the famous old forts, toured Old San Juan, and wound up at the huge Bacardi rum factory which, with its large outside pavilion and spacious, beautiful grounds, was a favorite Sunday spot not only for the people who worked weekdays in the plant, but for San Juan residents in general.

The big outdoor bar featured all kinds of rum drinks on the house. Their driver urged them to participate, and mainly to satisfy him they each had a piña colada and wandered around the grounds as they sipped it, looking across an inlet at a magnificent vista of Old San Juan.

Their driver told them that all varieties of Bacardi rum could be bought at the cheapest possible prices in a souvenir shop that was part of the factory complex.

Jo bypassed the rum, but bought a bright yellow T-shirt emblazoned with a huge black bat, the Bacardi symbol, to give to Tim.

Then the moment came to pack and head for the airport.

Alex had made arrangements with the same taxi driver. They were mostly silent as their cab wended its way through a constant stream of Sunday traffic to the Luis Muñoz Marín International Airport. Alex left first, and Jo followed shortly thereafter.

Her flight to Miami was booked solid. She was jammed into a seat between an enormous man and a very fat lady, and she felt like a squashed sardine by the time she disembarked. By the time she reached Sarasota, reclaimed first her baggage and then her car, she felt as if all the energy she possessed had been totally drained out of her.

Getting back to her condo was an enormous letdown. She'd closed the windows and shut off the air-conditioning before she left, so the apartment was both stuffy and stifling.

Jo switched the air-conditioning to Max, then took a long, cool shower. She felt so... bruised. Responsible for the troubled look in Alex's blue-gray eyes as he'd given her a last, long glance at the airport after kissing her goodbye.

Had she really disappointed him that intensely? Jo curled up on her couch and brooded, but she was too tired to come to any valid conclusions.

It was a further letdown to go back to work in the morning. She'd expected to walk into the office with a glow in her eyes that immediately would alert Marge to how wonderful her weekend had been. Instead, she was dragging herself along. To make matters much, much worse, Alex had not called last night.

As she walked into the office, Marge ran from her desk to grab her and hug her fiercely.

"Dear God, I'm glad you're safe!" Marge exclaimed.

While Jo was trying to recover from her surprise at this greeting, Bruce Chapman appeared in the doorway. "Wow!" Bruce declared. "Am I ever glad to see you! When I first heard about that plane crash, I was scared to death you might be involved."

Jo blanched. It took her a minute to rally enough to ask hoarsely, "What plane crash?"

"It turned out to be a New York-bound plane," Marge put in.

"The story's in the morning paper," Bruce interjected.

Jo reminded herself that Alex had left San Juan before she had. Nevertheless, her hands were shaking as she clutched the first section of the *Sarasota Herald Tribune*. The story, headed "Near-Fatal Crash at San Juan Airport," was in a front page box.

The accident, Jo read, had involved a New York-bound jet that had been delayed before takeoff for a further mechanical check. The problem, whatever it was, had been solved. The big jet had then been cleared for takeoff and was taxiing down the field when a small plane that had just landed took a wrong turn directly into its path. The pilot of the New York-bound jet had swerved to avert a collision, but he'd sheered off the wing of the smaller plane. The pilot of the small plane had been killed in the impact.

The article stated that there were at least thirty injured among the jet passengers, some of them seriously.

If anything had happened to Alex's plane, wouldn't she have been aware of it before her own takeoff? she asked herself. Wouldn't her own flight have been delayed because of the crash?

But logic told her the plane could well have been Alex's. It was the same airline he'd been flying, and that could be the reason why he hadn't phoned. Maybe Alex was lying in a San Juan hospital right now....

Jo sat down abruptly in the chair next to Marge's desk.

Alarmed, Marge said, "You've gone as white as a sheet. What is it, Jo?"

"It could have been Alex's plane." Jo's voice was little more than a whisper. "He was supposed to leave just a few minutes before I did. He said he'd call me from New York last night. He never did. Oh, Marge..."

"Bruce," Marge instructed, "the number of Malls International in New York is in that phone file on my desk. Call and ask for an Andrew Carson, will you? Tell him you're calling for Josephine Bennett. Then say Miss Bennett is concerned...."

Concerned. Marge's instructions to Bruce faded out as Jo latched onto that word. *Concerned*. That was the understatement of the year!

Faintly she heard Bruce say, "Mr. Carson? Bruce Chapman here at Greenscapes, Inc. in Sarasota. I'm Josephine Bennett's assistant. Miss Bennett's just heard about the plane crash in Puerto Rico and she's concerned about Mr. Grant. Yes, I see...."

Bruce covered the mouthpiece with his hand and turned to Jo. "Do you want to speak to Mr. Carson about this yourself?" he asked her.

Jo stood and went over to Marge's desk. Her knees were behaving like a couple of pieces of twisted rubber. She clutched the receiver, almost afraid to speak into it. "Andy?" she asked fearfully.

"Alex is okay, Jo," Andy Carson said quickly. "A little shaken up, a bump on his forehead and a few bruises, but he's okay. He was treated at the hospital in San Juan last night and released. He's probably on his way back to New York right now, and I'm sure you'll be hearing from him as soon as he gets to the office."

"Please," Jo said shakily. "Please ask him to call me, Andy."

The rest of that morning passed in a daze. Jo retreated to her own office, asked Marge to defer all calls until one came from Alex, and spent most of the time sitting at her desk with her head in her hands.

Suppose Alex had been killed last night? Suppose that farewell kiss at the airport had been their last?

She thought about the way she'd prattled on about work all the time. What had she been trying to prove? Herself? Had she really needed to prove herself to Alex in that fashion?

She doubted it. She knew that right now she didn't care whether or not Alex was the most successful businessman in the world. What she cared about was *Alex*.

A knock at her door shook her out of her reverie. Bruce stood in the doorway, grinning widely.

"I had to interrupt you, Jo," he said. "If your call comes through, I'll cut right out. But I've got to tell you Greenscapes has just won the Designers International award of the year for the Mimosa Mall plantscape."

"What?" Jo found it too difficult to switch gears quickly.

"A call just came through from the Designers International publisher," Bruce reported. "I took it since you didn't want any calls except Alex Grant's."

He paused triumphantly.

"Jo, you won *the* big award!" Bruce said jubilantly. "The ceremony is in New York, about the middle of September. There'll be papers from all over covering the banquet, as well as all our competition." Bruce grinned. "Miss Josephine Bennett, do you realize how famous you're going to be?"

Jo tried to work up some enthusiasm to show Bruce. The Designers International award was highly coveted. From this point on, she could pretty well write her own ticket.

Even a few days ago, knowing that would have been such a *trip*, she thought unhappily. Now it didn't matter very much. All that mattered was hearing from Alex. After a few appropriate remarks she managed to escort Bruce out of her office. Then she began brooding again.

Where *was* Alex?

Finally she couldn't stand it any longer. She dialed his New York office and asked for Andy, but it was

Andy's secretary who came on the line to say that Mr. Carson was in conference.

"I have to talk to him," Jo said desperately. "Please. This is urgent. Tell him it's Jo Bennett on the wire, and it's about Alex Grant. I—"

"Just a minute, Miss Bennett," the secretary said. A moment later Jo heard a familiar husky voice speak her name.

"Alex?" She clutched the phone receiver.

"Sweetheart, Andy's with me here in my office. I got in not ten minutes ago. He was just telling me you wanted me to call you, and I was just about to pick up the phone."

"It doesn't matter," Jo said swiftly. "Are you all right? That's all I want to know."

"Sure I'm all right," Alex told her. "That's to say—"

"Alex!" Shaken by the worry she'd been going through ever since walking into her office that morning, Jo suddenly felt sure he was holding something back from her. "Alex, please. If there's something wrong, tell me. Were you hurt?"

"Jo, I swear I'm all right," Alex said. "I got a cut on the head—"

"Andy didn't say that," Jo blurted frantically.

"Well, he didn't know it," Alex said calmly. "It's no big deal, just a couple of stitches. The main problem was that they gave me a sedative at the hospital last night and told me to take another pill once I got on my flight today. I hadn't eaten much, so it just about knocked me out. I was so bleary when I got to New York that I went right to my apartment and just about passed out for four hours. Otherwise you'd have heard from me a lot sooner."

"I've been so worried," Jo said, her voice still quavery.

"I thought you probably wouldn't connect the accident with my flight," Alex admitted, "or I would have called you from San Juan, regardless of the hour. Your plane took off just about the time we were back at the jetway rechecking a couple of things.

"When we hit that other plane," Alex added, "it was...one hell of a moment. They say your whole life flashes before you when you think you only have a couple of minutes left to live. But all I could see was you. All I could think about was what a mess we'd made out of our weekend together."

"I know," Jo said unhappily. "It wasn't your fault, Alex. It was mine."

"No, it wasn't," he cut in. "I should have had the sense not to start taunting you about your business. I know how hard you've worked, Jo. It was unfair of me to start digging you."

"But I didn't have to talk about Greenscapes all through dinner. Oh, Alex..."

She heard Alex say, "Yes?" and realized someone must have entered his office. She waited impatiently and heard him utter an exclamation that sounded as though he was pleased about something.

"Jo!" he exclaimed into the phone. "How absolutely terrific!"

She had no idea what he was talking about.

"The Designers International award," he prodded. "Andy just heard you won it!" Alex could not have sounded more enthusiastic. "That's a big plum for

Greenscapes," he told her. "You're going to be right in the front of the foliage field. And it's not going to do Mimosa Mall any harm, either. Andy tells me the banquet's here in September."

"Yes," Jo said, and wondered if her indifference was being conveyed to him with that one small word.

Evidently it wasn't, because Alex laughed and said, "Well! That'll be one way of luring you to my city, won't it?"

One way of luring her to his city. The more Jo thought about that remark of Alex's later, the more it annoyed her. And at the same time posed a real question. Was Alex saying that it wasn't on his schedule for them to meet again until mid-September? Nearly two months from now?

She stayed late at the office that afternoon, trying to catch up for what had essentially been a wasted day. It was hot and humid when she finally left, and she felt wilted just walking from the office to her car.

Suddenly she couldn't face going back to the empty condo. She drove out to a big shopping center complex where there was a choice of six different cinemas, and selected a picture she'd been wanting to see for quite a while. The movie had been an award-winner. Jo hoped it would provide an escape route for her for a couple of hours.

It didn't. She couldn't blame her restlessness on the movie. Right now she was entirely her own enemy, she knew.

It was nearly eleven when she got home, and as she entered the condo her telephone was ringing. She raced across the room to answer it but was a second too late.

When she picked up the receiver, she heard only a dial tone.

Had it been Alex? She would have thought he'd have been asleep by now, letting the effects of both the sedatives and the shock wear off.

Nevertheless, she nearly dialed New York, pausing only at the last instant. Suppose it hadn't been Alex, and she woke him up? Suppose it had been Alex? They just seemed to go around in circles every time they talked to each other.

Ten minutes later the phone rang again. It was Tim, and when he confessed it was he who had called earlier Jo was glad she hadn't yielded to impulse and dialed Alex, after all.

"Coz, I want to congratulate you, for one thing," Tim said. "The word about the award is all over the place. You must be pretty thrilled."

"Yes, it's great," Jo said dully.

"That's supposed to sound like you're thrilled?" Tim queried. "What's wrong?"

"I'm sort of tired, that's all."

"Yeah, I phoned Marge when I couldn't get you earlier, just to be sure you weren't off on one of those branch treks of yours, and she said you'd spent the weekend in Puerto Rico. You're not thinking about opening a branch in San Juan, are you?"

"No. That was supposed to be a holiday," Jo told him.

"I was just going to say that if you *were* planning a Puerto Rican operation, maybe you should transfer me," Tim announced airily. "The future Mrs. Timothy Bennett speaks Spanish fluently."

"The future Mrs. Timothy Bennett?"

"I nearly told you about her when you were over here," Tim confessed. "But she hadn't said yes, yet. Jo, I met her about two days after we opened the office here. Burdine's was having a sale of sport shirts and I stopped in around lunchtime to take a look. She was doing the selling. I hung around enough to buy six shirts from her."

Jo smiled despite herself. "Tim, you have to be kidding."

"Nope, I'm deadly serious," Tim informed her cheerfully. "She's part Cuban and part Scottish and when it comes to beauty she's a close runner-up to you, Coz."

"Tim, come on now," Jo protested.

"I mean that. And she speaks better English than I do." Tim lowered his voice and said more seriously, "I hope the two of you are going to like each other, Jo. You know how much you mean to me. It's important to me that you and Carmen hit it off."

He added, sounding more like Tim, "We're planning on an early September wedding. We thought maybe we'd head north for our honeymoon so we could catch up with you in New York for the awards banquet. But I want you to meet her sooner Jo. Like this weekend. Want to fly over to Miami?"

"Why don't you come here?" Jo suggested. "We can have a celebration dinner at my place Saturday night. I'd like that. As a matter of fact, you two can stay here. I can use the upstairs room at the office."

When she was remodeling, Jo had converted one of the upstairs rooms in the former farmhouse into what she called the R and R room. There was a studio couch, even a TV, so that she, or any employee, for that matter, could have a place to relax occasionally.

"We could stay at the office," Tim said. "I want to show her the nurseries, want her to see the whole Greenscapes operation. I'd sort of like to bring her into the business at some point, Jo. She's extremely smart, and I think she'd be a real asset. But there's plenty of time for all that."

They finished the conversation with the agreement that Tim would call once he'd made flight reservations, and Jo would meet him and his fiancée at the airport on Saturday.

Having the celebration to plan for helped Jo through the week. Alex called her a couple of times, but usually when he was on his way to a meeting, so their conversations weren't too satisfactory. She told him about the planned Saturday night celebration, and he said he hoped sometime to meet Tim, and his fiancée as well.

Jo made up a small party list for Saturday night, including the Baxters, Marge and her husband, Len Faraday, Bruce Chapman and a couple of other Greenscapes employees who'd been close to Tim. Everyone on the list knew Tim well, except for Bruce. Jo realized that she was pretty well asking Bruce for herself. Not as a date, exactly, but Bruce was fun and attractive. It would be nice to have a young man around to help her with the drinks and such.

To Tim's obvious pleasure, Jo and Carmen took to each other instantly. Carmen had a shock of black hair, bright blue eyes, and was just slightly on the plump side but very pretty. And there was no doubt in Jo's mind that she and Tim were very much in love.

She was happy for them, but couldn't help feeling a little bit sorry for herself as she dressed for the party that evening in a stunning, strapless white dress.

She'd packed a few things in a small suitcase that she stashed in the trunk of her car so that she could slip away once the guests had left, and let Tim and Carmen have her condo.

The party was a big success. There was only one bad moment when someone put on one of the Danny Forth tapes that had gotten mixed up with Jo's other tapes the night she'd played it for Alex. She shuddered when she heard that long-ago familiar voice, closed her eyes tightly, then stood so stiffly that Bruce, coming up behind her, asked, "Something wrong, Jo? You're not sick, are you?"

Sick at heart, she thought, but aloud she said, "No, I'm fine."

She imagined Bruce must remember Danny Forth. He was the right age. But if so, he didn't say anything.

Finally, the last person departed, and Jo quickly followed suit.

The nursery grounds were floodlighted at night, but still there were spooky shadows. Clutching her small suitcase, Jo unlocked the front door, switched on some lights, and made her way upstairs. She'd remembered to make up the studio couch as a bed before leaving for the airport. Now she was glad she had. All of a sudden, she was dead tired.

She slipped on a short, sheer cotton nightie, switched out all the lights, and slipped between the sheets. At long last she drifted off to sleep, but it was an uneasy sleep. Once she woke with a start and would have sworn she'd heard a car. If she had, though, the sound had probably come from a nearby highway. The air was humid and heavy that night, and sounds carried easily.

Jo went back to sleep again, then suddenly awakened and sat up, her pulse pounding.

There was someone downstairs.

She heard an object crash to the ground and froze. *Too late,* she told herself, she should have switched on the office security system before she went to bed.

There was no moon. It was pitch-dark, and Jo had not thought to provide herself with a flashlight. She edged out of bed, cautiously crept across the floor, and wished she'd had the foresight to put in an upstairs phone when she was doing her conversion.

Her only chance, she told herself, was to try to slip noiselessly downstairs and get to Marge's desk to dial the police.

Her foot was on the top step, when suddenly the whole house blazed with lights.

The intruder had found the light switches, and she stood fully revealed to him. No place to hide. Then she nearly collapsed from sheer amazement.

Alex stood at the foot of the staircase scowling up at her. "This is one hell of a fortress," he snarled. "Any damned fool could get in, though I nearly broke my neck trying to find a light I could turn on."

A white Band-Aid crossed the upper edge of Alex's forehead. It gave him a rakish look. He was wearing khaki shorts and a pale blue shirt and his dark hair was slightly rumpled. Jo suspected that he'd tripped and gone down when the chair—or whatever it was that had crashed—had met its fate.

Alex gave her a long, level look. "I suppose," he said, "you're going to ask me how I got here. Well, even though you weren't polite enough to ask me to come down for your cousin's engagement party, I decided to come anyway."

Jo opened her mouth, then closed it again. It had never occurred to her that he'd *want* to come to her party for Tim.

"However," Alex went on, "once again I picked the wrong flight. We were held for over two hours in Washington. Then it took forever to get a rental car at the airport. After which I naturally assumed you'd be in your own condo, and so that's where I went. Fifteen minutes later," he added with a grin, "I strongly suspect Tim and Carmen would have been in bed.

"So I introduced myself. I'd brought along a bottle of champagne, and they insisted we open it and drink a few toasts right on the spot. So we did. Including one to you, in absentia. Then Tim told me where you were, gave me his key to the building, and..." He shrugged. "Here I am."

Jo stared down at him, not knowing what to say.

"Well," he demanded huskily, "are you going to invite me to come up?"

Jo met him halfway down the stairs.

Chapter Fifteen

You don't suppose, do you, that the magic works only in Florida?" Alex asked innocently.

"Of course not!" Jo retorted.

"What makes you so certain of that?"

"Us," said Jo. "The magic has to do with us. It has nothing to do with geography."

They were in Alex's suite at the Floridiana, lying side by side on his supersized bed. They'd moved to the hotel just about the time daylight was spreading tentative fingers over Sarasota. They'd sailed majestically through the lobby, nodding affably to the sleepy-eyed clerk on duty at the registration desk, who had quickly and professionally masked his surprise.

They'd hastily thrown on their clothes and it was obvious. Alex was beginning to need a shave, and Jo had never seen his dark hair so disheveled. Her own hair was swirling wildly around her shoulders, her dress was mussed . . . and she couldn't have cared less. The important thing was that the stars had been glued back in their rightful places in the heavens and the moon was up there where it belonged. True, Jo couldn't *see* either the moon or the stars now that the rising sun in the east was taking over. But she knew they were there, exactly where they should be . . . and all was right with the world.

She'd always think about that little room up on the second floor of the farmhouse as the place where she and Alex had entered into a new dimension.

It had been quite a while before Alex had muttered, "I could use something with a little more sprawling space than this studio couch."

Jo chuckled. "Starting to get grouchy again, are you?" she teased him.

"What do you mean, again?"

"Oh, I don't know," she said, grinning impishly. "Now that you've mended your fences, shall we say, you want to move on to more comfortable quarters."

"Mended *my* fences? Seems to me you did a fair bit of the mending yourself, woman," Alex growled, and promptly took her in his arms. And they made love all over again.

Then they'd decided to move on to the Floridiana. Maybe even to take a sunrise swim, if the pool area wasn't closed off. But more important matters had intervened.

Lying by Alex's side, Jo had experienced a rare sense not only of peace, but of deep thankfulness. She still shuddered when she thought about the plane accident.

Alex turned toward her, his blue-gray eyes questioning. "What is it, sweetheart?" he asked her.

"Every now and then I remember that if...if things had been otherwise, you might not be here," Jo told him, and inadvertently shuddered again.

He said huskily, "You wouldn't get rid of me that easily."

"Alex, it's not something to joke about," she protested. "You'll never know what I went through when I heard about that accident. Then found out it was *your* plane...."

"I think I know exactly what you went through," Alex said quietly. "Because I know exactly what I'd have gone through if our roles had been reversed."

He cleared his throat and drew a deep breath. Then he asked, "Have I ever told you how very much I love you?"

Jo heard those age-old, three magic words and her eyes filled with tears.

He leaned over her and carefully kissed away the tears that were trembling on her lashes. Jo, opening her eyes, saw to her astonishment that his own were more than a little misty.

"I see you're wearing the little Aladdin's lamp I gave you," he said.

"Yes. I haven't taken it off except—"

"Except when you went to Puerto Rico," he finished for her.

Surprised, she said, "You noticed."

"Of course I noticed. I notice everything about you. And I admit I looked for the Aladdin's lamp because...well, it had come to have a crazy significance to me. Anyway, how could you possibly expect your personal genie to do anything for you if you didn't have a lamp to rub?"

Jo knew Alex was trying to handle the subject with a light touch, but she sensed a deep significance behind his words. It was another surprise. She wouldn't have thought it mattered to him.

She said, "I took the chain off when I was taking a shower not long before I had to leave for the airport. In my hurry, I forgot to put it on again. I felt...well, I felt lost without it. I tried to tell myself I was being ridiculously superstitious. But believe me, when things didn't work out between us I wished I had my little gold lamp to rub."

"What would you have wished for, Jo?" Alex asked softly.

She hesitated. Sometimes it wasn't easy to verbalize deep feelings. And this was something that went very deep. Slowly she said, "I would have wished for you. Though just then I would have had to wish for even more than that. I would have had to wish that we could somehow clear away the—well, I guess you'd call them the problems between us. I think of them more as blocks—impediments that were suddenly thrown up and that we just didn't seem to be able to get around in San Juan. I'd still say it was my fault."

Alex shook his head. "No, not really. I was equally to blame."

"I don't know," Jo said with a sigh. "It didn't matter, anyway. I guess it sometimes takes something major to make a person stop...take a real look at what's going on and reevaluate. Especially the way people live today they—we—tend to get priorities mixed up.

"When...when I was so afraid you'd been seriously hurt," she said, not quite able to bring herself to use the word "killed," "I knew that nothing I'd considered important till then was important at all, in comparison." She swallowed hard. "I would have given up Greenscapes and everything connected with it just to..."

Her voice failed her. Alex was still lying on his side, propped up on an elbow. Tenderly, very tenderly, he questioned, "Just to what, Jo?"

"To have you safe with me," Jo finished.

To her surprise, he sat up and swung his legs over the side of the bed. As she watched, he put on his shorts and strode to the window. She studied his back, wishing she could read his mood—and his mind—from his stance.

Jo got up, slipped on her robe and went over to his side. They looked across the hotel grounds and the wide boulevard that ran in front of the property to the harbor.

Almost timidly Jo touched Alex's arms, and he swung around to face her. She couldn't read his expression and, daunted, she asked, "What is it?"

"A while back," he answered, "I told you something I've never said to another woman. But you didn't really answer me."

When Jo looked at him uncomprehendingly, he added gently, "I told you I love you, Jo. Those are words you've never said to me."

She drew back, startled. "Do you doubt I love you?" she demanded. "Didn't I just tell you that when I feared for your safety the only thing in the world that mattered to me was having you safe?"

"That's not quite the same thing," Alex stated levelly. "Can't you say it, Jo?"

"Say it? Could anything be more obvious, Alex?" A smile curved Jo's lips. She said softly, "This is the

easiest thing you've ever asked of me, or probably ever
will. Yes, I love you. I love you, love you, *love you*.
My heart's so full of my love for you it's a wonder it
doesn't spill over...."

Jo felt Alex's muscles tighten under her touch, and
she stepped back, her smile fading as she stared up into
his face. Then he said unsteadily, "I don't think you
know how much this means to me."

"What are you saying?"

"I've been scared ever since I met you that I might
lose something I'd just found. That's been one of our
big problems. Not you. Me."

"I haven't exactly been not scared, Alex," Jo told
him.

Alex shook his head unhappily. "God, I'm saying
this badly," he confessed.

"Just what *are* you trying to say, Alex?"

"I guess that maybe I'm afraid you sort of—well,
sort of lost your sense of perspective, because of the
plane accident."

"What's that supposed to mean?"

"I can't imagine you ever considering giving up
Greenscapes, if the chips were really down," Alex told
her seriously. "I think that's sort of an—well, an illusion on your part, Jo. I can understand how you felt
that way when you heard about the plane accident.
But that was emotionalism. Frankly, I think no matter what had happened, once you simmered down
you'd want Greenscapes back."

Jo stared at him, the hurt showing on her face. Alex
grimaced. "Hey!" he protested. "Please, Jo. Don't
take what I'm saying the wrong way. I just don't want
our future built on shifting sands, that's all."

Jo turned away. "I don't know what to say to you," she admitted.

Alex touched her shoulder imploringly. "Sweetheart," he said huskily, "I just want it to be right between us, don't you see? It's better for both of us if we're totally honest."

"I was being totally honest, Alex," she told him, beginning to feel very tired. Tired, and frustrated.

"I know you think you were. I'm just asking you to take another look now that you *have* me by your side, safe and sound. Could you still honestly tell me you wouldn't mind giving up Greenscapes?"

She faced him. "Are you asking me to give you Greenscapes?"

Alex's lips tightened. "I wouldn't be that presumptuous, Jo," he said quietly.

"Alex, what am I supposed to tell you?" Jo was trying to appeal to his sense of fair play. "All right, it *would* be difficult for me to sell Greenscapes tomorrow morning. But what I was saying was—"

"I know what you were saying. You were willing to bargain with fate. Wasn't that it?"

There was no rancor in his voice. But there was a heaviness that struck at Jo. She obviously still wasn't giving him the answers he needed.

She sighed. "I think I'm going to take a shower and get some clothes on," she announced.

"Want to take a swim?" Alex suggested. He was looking out the window again. "There are a couple of early birds in the pool," he observed.

"Thanks, no. You go ahead if you want to."

"Maybe I will. I don't know. Jo, look..."

Jo was at the bedroom door. She turned. "Yes?"

"I'm not asking you to give up Greenscapes," Alex said. "You've worked too hard, it means too much to you. I want you to understand that."

Jo shook her head, her expression wry. "You're not asking me to give up Greenscapes, yet if I keep it we're never going to have much of a future together, are we?" she asked him.

"That's not necessarily so."

"Oh, Alex," Jo pleaded, "let's be honest with each other. It's my business that's come between us and caused all the difficulties and misunderstandings we've had. Don't you think I realize that? Fair or not, that's the way it is, and will always be as long as I remain president of Greenscapes. And yes, you're right. I don't want to step down. I was completely honest when I said I would have been more than willing to give it all up to have you safe. Call that bargaining with fate, if you like. But I meant it. I would mean it again, if you were in danger. But you're right, under normal circumstances so much does look different." Helplessly, Jo finished, "I just don't know."

She turned and headed for the bathroom. But even a long shower wasn't enough to wash away the feeling of defeat that was encroaching, had been encroaching ever since Alex had started bringing up the subject of Greenscapes.

He seemed to consider her business a rival, which was ridiculous. Surely he must realize she had room in her life for both a business and a deep personal involvement? The reasons why he hadn't had deep personal involvements over the years had nothing to do with her ability to carry on both a successful business and private life. He knew that. Didn't he?

She dressed in a cool pink cotton sheath she'd taken to the farmhouse the previous night, slipped on flat white sandals, and went out to face Alex again. He'd put on bathing trunks, she saw, and he said rather unhappily, "I think I will go down and take a swim."

"Is it okay to swim while you still have that cut on your head?" She knew his stitches hadn't yet been taken out.

"I'll keep my head out of the water." He paused. "Want me to order up some breakfast for you first?"

"No. There's instant coffee in your kitchenette. I may brew myself a cup. But it's too early to think about eating."

Alex surveyed her ruefully. "I don't know why I consistently make such a mess of things with you," he admitted. "I guess maybe it's because I care so much. Jo..."

"Yes?"

"Please don't run away."

She looked at him, surprised. "I have no intention of running away."

"What I'm saying is, please don't go off while I'm swimming. I need to count on your being here when I get back."

There was an urgency in his tone that puzzled her.

"I'll be here," she said.

"That's a promise?"

"Yes, it's a promise."

With Alex gone, Jo went to the kitchenette and made herself a cup of coffee. She drank it standing up.

The telephone rang, and she automatically glanced at the clock next to it. Not quite eight on a Sunday morning? Was Alex being called from New York on business?

She picked up the phone. Alex said huskily, "Jo?"

"Where are you?" she asked, momentarily alarmed.

"I'm at a phone in the lobby. I don't know what the hell came over me up there a few minutes ago. I don't know why I turn so *stupid* sometimes when I'm around you. If I ran my business the way I've been trying to handle *you* I'd have gone bankrupt a long time ago."

She had to laugh, then said rather shakily, "I guess that makes two of us."

"Sweetheart, look, let me say once and for all what never seems to come out clearly if you're around. I'll never ask you to give up Greenscapes. But I am asking you to let me into your life. I mean...on a permanent basis."

Jo could feel her pulse accelerating.

"I know," Alex continued, "that it would be rough on you to handle at long distance a business plus a husband who'd be as demanding as I'll probably be. I know you can't move Greenscapes. But I *can* move Malls International."

"Alex, can you...are you saying...?" Jo gasped.

"There's no reason why headquarters has to be in New York," Alex pointed out. "We could just as well set up here in Sarasota. We would function with equal efficiency.

"That's one reason," he went on, "why I was so interested in looking at property around here. I want a house on Siesta Key for my—for our—own private use, yes. But I was also looking around for a business site. Fred's been looking for me, too."

"Fred Baxter?" Jo could not have been more astonished.

"Yes. Fred's come up with a couple of excellent potential sites," Alex informed her. "I've talked to Andy about this, and he's more than willing to make the move, as would be a number of others on my staff. We'd continue to maintain a New York City office, though, and those who don't want to make the move south can hold the fort there."

Jo said weakly, "You sound like this is something you've already given the green light to."

"No," Alex admitted after a moment. "Not entirely. A yellow light, yes. But technically, yellow's a light of caution. And especially after Puerto Rico, I admit I became pretty...cautious. Now..."

"Yes?"

"I want *you* to be sure, Jo."

"Will you believe me if I say I am?"

"I don't know," Alex confessed unhappily. "Sweetheart, I can only ask you to forgive me for seeming to be such a skeptic. It isn't that I don't trust you and believe in you, because I do. But I have to be sure that you have room for me, Jo. I need so much from you."

Jo didn't know how to answer him. Of course she had room for him. And she had so much to give him. Her love for him poured out as she thought about it. But he had to believe that. He had to put his faith in her, just as she'd be putting her faith in him. That was part of a real commitment between two people. She was ready to make it fully. All she had to do was convince him.

"Jo?" Alex asked.

"Yes."

"Look," he said, "a while back in New York, before that weekend in Puerto Rico, I made something for you. I took it to San Juan, but the way things went I decided that wasn't the time to give it to you. But I brought it with me. It's, well, it's in the top drawer of that chest in the bedroom. You won't miss it. I want you to get it and . . . and do the obvious.''

"Do the obvious?" she echoed.

"Yes. Just humor me, will you, sweetheart. And later I'll catch up with you.''

With that, Alex hung up. Mystified, Jo slowly followed suit. Almost reluctantly she went into the bedroom and opened the top drawer of the chest, more than half afraid of what she was going to find.

She saw a small cassette recorder and, next to it, a tape. Still mystified, she picked up the tape and scanned it for some identification. There wasn't any. Which meant that Alex had, literally, made this tape.

She was almost afraid to discover what he'd put on it.

She took the recorder and the tape back into the living room and sat down. Only then did she load the recorder and press the Play button.

She heard the strum of guitar chords, the fingering of a melody she'd never heard before, yet it was immediately haunting. It was the kind of music Danny Forth had once played.

But this wasn't Danny she was hearing, she realized; it was Alex singing to her. As she listened to him, she heard qualities in his husky voice that Danny Forth had never had. Maturity. Depth of emotion.

As she listened to the words, she knew Alex had written this song for her. It was his ultimate declaration of love. Through the music that was so much a part of him—and now denied him—he was telling her things he still couldn't say in any other way.

"I walked with loneliness
I lived with loneliness
A gray lady in a shabby dress
Always with me, blotting out the world.

"And then I saw you
standing between the sunlight and the shadows
I saw you and your beauty beckoned.
And when I followed, the gray lady turned and
went away.

"This is a new world you've opened to me,
sweetheart
Your world, my world, a new world.
Can I hold it in my hands?
Can I keep it in my heart?

"Or...will you leave me?
And will the gray lady in the shabby dress return?
Will she clutch me, until I can never let her go
again?
Will I walk with loneliness?
Will I live with loneliness?
As I have since my time began.
until you came between the sunlight and the
shadows
and gave me love."

By the time Alex had strummed the final chord,
tears were streaming down Jo's face. She went back to
Alex's dresser and borrowed a couple of his handker-
chiefs, and soon they were sodden. She turned the tape
on again and huddled in the chair listening—until the
tears stopped and she could hear and at last begin to
know how much she meant to him.

Then she recalled that Marge had tabbed Alex as a lonely man. She had disagreed. How could a man so rich, so handsome, so successful, be lonely? she'd asked.

Well, now she knew. *Will I live with loneliness? As I always have, since my time began.*

"Oh, my darling, no," Jo murmured brokenly. "No. Never, never again!"

Finally she took the tape out of the recorder and put it back in its box. She dried her eyes for the last time, and sponged her face with cold water until the emotion she'd been pouring out wasn't quite so obvious.

Resolutely she went out to the elevator and pressed the button for the pool area. As she rode down it struck her that Alex, in making that tape, had gone against his doctor's advice. It was something he shouldn't have done...but, just this once, she couldn't help but be glad that he had.

She walked towards the pool, scanning it for Alex. He was in the water, swimming furiously, like a man possessed. She watched him cut through the water with his long, powerful arms as if he felt that by exhausting himself he could work out all his fears and frustrations.

She stood watching him, and when he reached the end of the pool he turned and saw her.

He was too far away for her to read his face distinctly, and as she watched him climb out of the water she decided she could wait no longer.

She sped around the pool toward him, slipping a couple of times on the wet tiles. She went into Alex's arms and hugged him fiercely.

She could feel the dampness of his bathing trunks against her dress. Rivulets of water were dripping from his wet skin onto her shoulders. Alex said huskily, "I'm soaking you."

Jo looked up at him and let her heart show. Later she could talk, later she could tell him how she felt about the song he'd written for her. How she wanted to spend the rest of her life with him. How she loved him. Oh, God, how she loved him!

But right now she let her actions speak louder than words. She reached up, tugged Alex's head toward her, and crushed her lips against his.

When at last she had to pause for breath, she whispered, "Oh my darling, my dearest . . . never doubt me."

She felt Alex tense for just a moment. Then he relaxed. She saw moisture in his blue-gray eyes that had nothing to do with his swim. He smiled, and Jo's own, personal sun came out. She didn't need to rub her little Aladdin's lamp and summon a genie to know that all she could ever wish for had just come true.

* * * * *

ATTRACTIVE, SPACE SAVING BOOK RACK

Display your most prized novels on this handsome and sturdy book rack. The hand-rubbed walnut finish will blend into your library decor with quiet elegance, providing a practical organizer for your favorite hard-or soft-covered books.

Only $9.95

Approximately 16" x 8" when assembled

Assembles in seconds!

To order, rush your name, address and zip code, along with a check or money order for $10.70* ($9.95 plus 75¢ postage and handling) payable to *Silhouette Books.*

Silhouette Books
Book Rack Offer
901 Fuhrmann Blvd.
P.O. Box 1396
Buffalo, NY 14269-1396

Offer not available in Canada.

*New York and Iowa residents add appropriate sales tax.

BKR-2A

CHILDREN OF DESTINY

A trilogy by Ann Major

Three power-packed tales of irresistible passion and undeniable fate created by Ann Major to wrap your heart in a legacy of love.

PASSION'S CHILD — September

Years ago, Nick Browning nearly destroyed Amy's life, but now that the child of his passion—the child of her heart—was in danger, Nick was the only one she could trust....

DESTINY'S CHILD — October

Cattle baron Jeb Jackson thought he owned everything and everyone on his ranch, but fiery Megan MacKay's destiny was to prove him wrong!

NIGHT CHILD — November

When little Julia Jackson was kidnapped, young Kirk MacKay blamed himself. Twenty years later, he found her...and discovered that love could shine through even the darkest of nights.

Don't miss PASSION'S CHILD, DESTINY'S CHILD and NIGHT CHILD, three thrilling Silhouette Desires designed to heat up chilly autumn nights!

SD-445

Silhouette Special Edition

COMING NEXT MONTH

#481 CHAMPAGNE FOR BREAKFAST—Tracy Sinclair
Raoul Ruiz, Mexico City's most eligible bachelor, generously salvaged
Lacey Scott's vacation. Then he passionately romanced her, proving as
intoxicating—and elusive—as the bubbles in a glass of champagne.

#482 THE PLAYBOY AND THE WIDOW—Debbie Macomber
More earthy than beautiful, more wholesome than sexy, housewife and
mother Diana Collins wasn't playboy Cliff Howard's type. So why did he
find the plucky widow irresistibly enticing?

#483 WENDY WYOMING—Myrna Temte
That heavenly voice! Who *was* Cheyenne, Wyoming's sexy new deejay?
Jason Wakefield pumped his pal, radio insider Melody Hunter—but
suddenly he wanted Mel more than the answer!

#484 EDGE OF FOREVER—Sherryl Woods
Dana Brantley had sacrificed intimacy for refuge from a traumatic,
haunting past. But insistent Nick Verone and his adorable ten-year-old son
kept pushing. Would the truth destroy their fragile union?

#485 THE BARGAIN—Patricia Coughlin
Vulnerable Lisa Bennett kept pursuers at bay, so wily Sam Ravenal played
hard to get. Intriguing her with pirate lore and hidden treasure, Sam freed
her anchored imagination . . . and baited her heart.

#486 BOTH SIDES NOW—Brooke Hastings
To buttoned-down Bradley Fraser, Sabrina Lang was reckless,
irresponsible . . . and dangerously alluring. Then, on a Himalayan
adventure, Brad spied her softer side—and fell wholeheartedly in love!

AVAILABLE NOW:

#475 SKIN DEEP
Nora Roberts

#476 TENDER IS THE KNIGHT
Jennifer West

#477 SUMMER LIGHT
Jude O'Neill

#478 REMEMBER THE DAFFODILS
Jennifer Mikels

#479 IT MUST BE MAGIC
Maggi Charles

#480 THE EVOLUTION OF ADAM
Pat Warren